ANOTHER WORLD

PAT BARKER

——————

ANOTHER WORLD

FARRAR, STRAUS AND GIROUX
NEW YORK

Farrar, Straus and Giroux
19 Union Squre West, New York 10003

Copyright ©1998 by Pat Barker
All rights reserved
Printed in the United States of America
First published in 1998 by Viking U.K.
First Farrar, Straus and Giroux edition, 1999
Second printing, 1999

For David, Donna and Gillon
– with love

Remember: the past won't fit
into memory without something left over;
it must have a future.

— JOSEPH BRODSKY

ANOTHER WORLD

ONE

Cars queue bumper to bumper, edge forward, stop, edge forward again. Resting his bare arm along the open window, Nick drums his fingers. The Bigg Market on a Friday night. Litter of chip cartons, crushed lager cans, a gang of lads with stubble heads and tattooed arms looking for trouble – and this is early, it hasn't got going yet. Two girls stroll past, one wearing a thin, almost transparent white cotton dress. At every stride her nipples show, dark circles beneath the cloth, fish rising. One of the lads calls her name: 'Julie!' She turns, and the two of them fall into each other's arms.

Nick watches, pretending not to.

> What is love's highest aim?
> Four buttocks on a stem.

Can't remember who said that – some poor sod made cynical by thwarted lust. Nothing wrong with the aim, as far as Nick can see – just doesn't seem much hope of achieving it any more. And neither will these two, or not yet. The boy's mates crowd round, grab him by the belt, haul him off her. 'Jackie-no-balls,' the other girl jeers. The boy thrusts his pelvis forward, makes wanking movements with his fist.

Lights still red. Oh, come on. He's going to be late, and he doesn't want to leave Miranda waiting at the station. This is her first visit to the new house. Fran wanted to put it off, but then Barbara went into hospital and that settled it. Miranda had to come, and probably for the whole summer. Well, he was pleased, anyway.

The lights change, only to change back to red just as he reaches the crossing. Should be easier in the new house – more space. In the flat Gareth's constant sniping at Miranda was starting to get on everybody's nerves. And Miranda never hit back, which always made him want to strangle Gareth, and then it was shouts, tears, banged doors: 'You're not my father . . . ' So who was? he wanted to ask. Never did, of course.

Green – thank God. But now there's a gang of lads crossing, snarled round two little buggers who've chosen this moment to start a fight. His fist hits the horn. When that doesn't work he leans out of the window, yells, 'Fuck off out of it, will you?'

No response. He revs the engine, lets the car slide forward till it's just nudging the backs of their thighs. Shaved heads swivel towards him. Barely time to get the window up before the whole pack closes in, hands with whitening fingertips pressed against the glass, banging on the bonnet, a glimpse of a furred yellow tongue, spit trapped in bubbles between bared teeth, noses squashed against the glass. Then, like a blanket of flies, they lift off him, not one by one, all at the same time, drifting across the road, indifferent now, too good-tempered, too sober to want to bother with him. One lad lingers, spoiling for a fight. 'Leave it, Trev,' Nick hears. 'Stupid old fart int worth it.'

He twists round, sees a line of honking cars, yells, 'Not my fucking fault!' then, realizing they can't hear him, jabs two fingers in the air. Turns to face the front. Jesus, the lights are back to red.

By the time he reaches the station he's twenty minutes late. Leaving the car in the short-stay car-park, he runs to the platform, only to find it deserted. He stands, staring down the curve of closed doors, while a fear he knows to be irrational begins to nibble at his belly. A few months ago a fourteen-year-old girl was thrown from a train by some yob who hadn't got anywhere when he tried to chat her up. Miranda's thirteen. This is all rubbish, he knows that. But then, like everybody else, he lives in the shadow of monstrosities. Peter Sutcliffe's bearded face, the number plate of a house in Cromwell Street, three figures smudged on a video surveillance screen, an older boy taking a toddler by the hand while his companion strides ahead, eager for the atrocity to come.

Think. Hot day, long journey, she'll fancy a coke, but

when he looks into the café he can't see her. The place is crowded, disgruntled bundles sipping orange tea from thick cups, shifting suitcases grudgingly aside as he edges between the tables. A smell of hot bodies, bloom of sweat on pale skins, like the sheen on rotten meat, God what a place. And then he sees her, where he should have known all along she would be, waiting sensibly beneath the clock, her legs longer and thinner than he remembers, shoulders hunched to hide the budding breasts. She looks awkward, gawky, Miranda who's never awkward, whose every movement is poised and controlled. He wants to rush up and kiss her, but stops himself, knowing this is a moment he'll remember as long as he's capable of remembering anything.

Then she catches sight of him, her face is transformed, for a few seconds she looks like the old Miranda. Only her kiss isn't the boisterous hug of even two months ago, but a grown-up peck delivered across the divide of her consciously hollowed chest.

Feeling ridiculously hurt, he picks up her suitcase, puts his other arm around her shoulder, and leads her to the car.

Fran becomes aware that Gareth has come into the room behind her. He moves quietly, and his eyes wince behind his glasses, no more than an exaggerated blink, but it tweaks her nerves, says: You're a lousy mother. Perhaps I am, she thinks. She's failed, at any rate, in what seems to be a woman's chief duty to her son: to equip him with a father who's more than a bipedal sperm bank. Of course she has supplied Nick, but he's bugger-all use. Fantastic with other people's problem kids, bloody useless with his own.

Back to the shopping list. Bran flakes, bumf, toothpaste, toothbrush in case Miranda's forgotten hers, air freshener, vinegar, potatoes . . . Something else. What the hell was it?

Gareth blinks again, breathing audibly through his mouth.

She's tired of the guilt, fed up to the back teeth with attributing every nervous tic, every piece of bad behaviour, every failed exam to the one crucial omission. Nobody knows. Suppose it wasn't the absence of a father, suppose it was the presence of two mothers? God knows her mother would sink anybody. And the alternative – which it suited everybody to forget – was the North Sea or the incinerator or whatever the bloody hell they did. And he'd come within a hair's breadth – literally – of that. Lying on the bed, already shaved, when she decided she couldn't go through with it. She started to cry, the gynaecologist hugged her – and later sent her a bill for 150 quid. Must've been the most expensive hug in history. And then she got up, walked down the long gleaming corridor, and out into the open air. She stood outside the phone box for half an hour, a cold wind blowing up her fanny, before plucking up the courage to ring Mark at work. Put on hold for five minutes, she fed ten pees she couldn't afford into the box, and listened to the theme song from *Dr Zhivago*. When Mark finally came on the line, he said, 'I knew you wouldn't go through with it.' Typical. Mark had to be in control, had to know what other people were going to do before they did. Later, in bed, he said, 'Fran, there's no need to worry. I'll marry you. I said I would and I will.' 'You needn't,' she said, pressing her hand over the place where the baby was. And he didn't. Gone before the hair grew back.

'Gareth, what do you *want?*'

Gareth's thinking how ugly she looks, with her great big bulge sticking out. He wonders what the baby looks like. Is it a proper baby with eyes and things or is it just a blob? He'd watched a brill video at Digger's house, when his mam and Teddy were still in bed. A woman gave birth to a maggot because her boyfriend had turned into a fly or something like that, he never really got the hang of it because Digger kept fast-forwarding to the good bits. And the maggot was all squashy when it came out, and they kept looking at each other to see who'd be the first to barf but nobody did.

'What are you staring at?' Fran asks sharply.

'Nothing.'

'Have you done your homework?'

'Yeah.'

'What was it?'

'When's she coming?'

'"She's" the cat's grandmother.'

'When's *Miranda* coming?'

A glance at the clock. 'They should be here now. What did you have to do?'

'The Great Fire of London.'

'I thought you'd done that.'

'Not with Miss Bailes. Why is she?'

'Why is she coming?' Fran hears herself repeat in a Joyce Grenfell comic-nanny sort of voice – she can't believe it's coming out of her mouth; this is what having kids does to you – 'Because it's her home.'

A derisory click of the tongue. Gareth edges closer, scuffing his sleeve along the table. In a moment he's going to touch her and, God forgive her, she doesn't want him to.

'What's wrong with Barbara?'

Fran opens her mouth to insist on some more respectful way of referring to Barbara, then closes it again. How *is* a child supposed to refer to its stepfather's first wife? 'Auntie' Barbara sounds silly. And 'Mrs Halford', though technically correct, doesn't sound right either. 'She's ill.'

'What sort of ill?'

Fran shrugs. 'Ill enough to be in hospital.'

'How long's she coming for?'

'Six weeks.'

'Shit.'

Yes, Fran thinks. Shit. 'I hope you're going to make

more of an effort this time, Gareth. You don't have to play together –'

'We don't "play".'

True, Fran thinks. Gareth's obsession with zapping billions of aliens to oblivion hardly seems to count as play. 'You'll have to be here to meet her when she comes, but –'

'Why?'

'Because I say so.'

He reaches her at last, rests his hand on her shoulder for a second while she sits motionless, enduring the contact. After a while the small warm thing is lifted off her and he goes away.

'Sorry I'm late,' Nick says, heaving Miranda's suitcase into the boot. 'Traffic's terrible.'

' 'S all right.'

He knows she's hoping for something to happen, a cup of tea, anything, to prolong the time alone with him before she has to face Fran and Gareth. Well, it can't be like that. 'Did you have a good journey?'

'All right.'

She gets in, clicks her seat belt. Sighs.

'Is term over?'

'I don't know. I missed the last few weeks.'

'Because of Mum?' Nick, craning to see over his shoulder, delays reversing. 'How is she?'

'Fine.'

He looks at her shuttered profile. By no possible standards can a woman confined to a psychiatric hospital for an indefinite period be described as 'fine', but then Miranda knows that. 'Fine' means: You no longer have the right to know.

'How's Grandad?' she asks.

'Not good. Operation tomorrow.'

A pause. Typical of Miranda that there's no automatic expression of sympathy. 'Will I be able to see him?'

'Maybe in a few days. He'll be pretty rough to begin with.' He glances sideways at her. 'Is Mum very bad?'

'No, she's fine.'

A pursing of the lips brings the conversation to a close. Though very shy, Miranda can be formidable. And perhaps she's justified in refusing to answer. What right *has* he to know? He remembers Barbara coming in from the garden one morning, complaining in that bright, jokey, hysterical way that somebody's been putting green fly on her roses. He and Miranda exchanged glances, in it together. And then, less than a year later, he moved out and Miranda realized that while she was in it for life, he was merely in it for the duration of the marriage.

'How's Fran?' Miranda asks politely.

'Fine.' For God's sake, we can't have everybody fine. 'Tired. Jasper's teething.' Jasper's always teething. It's like hand-rearing a great white shark.

'Has Gareth broken up?'

'Not yet, day after tomorrow.'

Miranda receives this information in silence. She and Gareth have not so far managed to hit it off, though they're at a stage when the sexes separate naturally; the hostility between them doesn't necessarily spring from personal dislike, or so Nick tells himself.

'Dad?'

'Hm?'

'Can I tell you a joke?'

'Yes, go on.' He's concentrating on the traffic.

'There's this fella and he gans to a pro and he says, "How much is a blow job?" and she says, "A tenner." So he turns out his pockets and he says, "Aw hell, I've only got the seven, what can I have for seven?" She says, "You can have a wank," so he gets his dick out and she looks down at it and she says, "Here, love, have a lend o' three quid."' A pause. 'Is that funny?'

'Yeah, quite. Where'd you get it from?'

'Man on the train.'

Oh yes. 'Was he a nice man?'

'All right. Bit drunk.'

If this is an attempt to divert him from asking questions about Barbara it's certainly succeeding.

'What do you call three blobs on a window pane?'

'Miranda –'

'Da-ad.'

'OK – what do you call three blobs on a window pane?'

'Condomsation.'

'Did he sit next to you all the way?'

'I got that one from school.'

He can't keep up with the changes in her. Even if they were still living together he'd probably be finding it difficult – apart, it's impossible. 'Not long now,' he says.

'Why's it called Lob's Hill?'

'Dunno. I keep meaning to look it up, but there's so many other things to do. We're not unpacked yet.'

They're driving through Summerfield. Here the streets run in parallel lines down to the river, to the boarded-up armaments factory, like a row of piglets suckling a dead sow. Before the First World War 25,000 local men worked in that factory. Now it employs a few thousand who drive in from estates on the outskirts of the city.

He never gets used to this, no matter how often he drives through it. Floorboards in the middle of the road, broken glass, burnt-out cars, charred houses with huge holes in the walls as if they've been hit by artillery shells. Beirut-on-Tyne, the locals call it.

The traffic lights are on red, but he doesn't stop. Nobody stops here. You slow down, but you don't stop. It's difficult not to slow down, there are so many traffic-calming devices: chicanes, bollards, sleeping policemen. Law-abiding motorists creep through at fifteen miles an hour. Joy riders, knocking the guts out of other people's cars, speed along this road like rally drivers.

Leaving it behind now, thank God. He picks up speed on the hill, the houses on either side increasing in prosperity with every mile that separates them from the estate. Huge Victorian houses built by iron magnates, shipbuilders, armaments manufacturers, well away from the sight and sound and smell of money. Most of them are divided into flats now. Lob's Hill is one of the few houses left that's still a family home.

As he turns into the drive, branches from overgrown bushes on either side rattle against the windows. The house is big, ugly, late Victorian, the turrets at either end surmounted by faintly ludicrous towers. Nick turns off the engine. He can feel Miranda not liking it.

'It's better inside,' he says.

She gets out, and stands on the gravel looking lost while he hauls her suitcase out of the boot. It's suddenly very quiet. Even the cawing of rooks from the copse behind the house seems to drop away.

A climbing rose covers the front of the building, though the white blooms are fading to brown, seeming to be not so much decayed as melted on their stems. It hasn't been pruned for years. At some stage a honeysuckle's been trained over the lower branches, but now it's died back to form a huge ball of dead wood and leaves, defended by the sharp thorns of the rose.

Yesterday Nick had spent the whole morning snipping away with the secateurs, hauling out dead twigs by the handful, tearing the skin on his arms till he looked as if he had some horrible disease. Once, thrusting his hand deep into the mass, he pulled out a blackbird's nest, full of dead fledglings. 'Gollies', they used to call them when he was a child. He looked at them, at the black spines of feathers pricking through the purplish skin, the sealed, bulbous eyes, the yellow wavy rim around the beaks, and then, with a spasm of revulsion, he threw the nest on to the wheelbarrow. But at least he'd managed to expose the lintel with its carved name and date. He looks up at the house now and points it out to Miranda.

FANSHAWE
1898

'Like Wuthering Heights,' she says.

Nick catches a movement behind one of the upstairs windows, a flash of light. Gareth's staring down at them, the sunlight glinting on his glasses. He doesn't smile or wave.

'Right, then,' Nick says, picking up the suitcase and putting his other arm around Miranda's shoulders. Together they go in.

TWO

Fran lifts saucepan lids, prods vegetables, each blast of steam leaving her hotter, stickier, more harassed than before. The potatoes have boiled dry; not disastrously, but they're going to taste 'caught'. There's something you can do about that. Mash them? She reaches for the *Cheat's Cookbook*. Yes, transfer them to a clean saucepan, mash them with full-cream milk and a knob of butter – she has neither, they're bad for Nick's heart – and cover lightly with 'an aromatic cloud of freshly grated nutmeg and a sprinkling of freshly chopped parsley'.

She can't help thinking anybody who could lay that on at a moment's notice had probably managed not to burn the potatoes in the first place. What *she* has is half a packet of mixed herbs, grey with age. The nutmeg's at the bottom of a packing case and the pots of fresh herbs got left behind in the flat. 'Shurrup, you,' she says to Jasper, ruffling his hair, amazed by the warmth of his scalp under her fingers. He's sitting on the floor at her feet, going 'broom broom' as he drives a dinky car up her leg. You wouldn't think he'd been awake half the night. Normally she'd have gone to bed with him, when he had his afternoon nap, but today she couldn't because of having to get bloody Miranda's bloody room ready.

Though she ought to be grateful there's a room to get ready. In the flat Miranda had slept on a camp bed in the living room. It was odd, that in the first days after the move, even though she had all this extra space, Fran tended to confine herself to a few rooms: the kitchen, the bedroom, the living room. Like a prisoner who takes one look at the sky and shelters in a shop doorway. She's getting more used to it now. The final months in that flat had almost broken her. It had been all right when Jasper was a baby because he didn't cry much, but as soon as he became a toddler the trouble started. The woman in the flat downstairs – nicknamed The Grum – was always banging on the ceiling. Fran went down and tried to talk about it, but she wasn't having any of that. Miss Hardcastle, her name was. She'd taken to tranquillizers in a big way after her mother died, and then, against her doctor's advice, had gone cold turkey on them. And poor woman, she was to be pitied, she was climbing up the wall. The slightest noise had her shouting and screaming and hammering on the ceiling and complaining to the landlord. On wet days, when Jasper had a cold, Fran would run a bath and sit in it with him, singing songs and reading stories and playing with boats. For hours, sometimes, because it was the only way to avoid another row. Once Nick came in from work to find her sitting in tepid water with tears streaming down her face. That was all behind her now, though. In this house Jasper can make any amount of noise. He can run about and trundle his car up and down the corridors to his heart's content. OK, it's a mess, there's a lot to do, and not much money to do it with, but they'd been right to move. Even when all the dashing about had sent her blood pressure sky high, she'd never doubted that. And they'd get through the decorating gradually, and at least in a house this size Miranda and Gareth won't be continually bickering. No, it's going to be good. She's looking forward to it.

Voices in the hall. 'Come on,' she says, picking Jasper up. 'Let's see your sister.'

They're in the living room, looking out into the garden.

'Hello, Miranda.'

There's a moment when Miranda clearly contemplates the hypocrisy of a kiss and rejects it. 'Hello, Fran. How are you?'

God, she's cool. Fran always thinks she remembers how cool Miranda is, and yet obviously she doesn't, because every time it comes as a shock. 'Not so bad. Glad the move's over.'

Miranda holds out her hand to Jasper, who pulls away from her, hiding his face in Fran's neck.

'He's tired,' Nick says quickly, to cover the slight awkwardness.

'Well,' says Fran. 'What do you think?'

'It's a lovely big room.'

'Of course we haven't started yet.' She nods at the wallpaper. 'That's the first job. I mean, can you imagine living with that? Enough to drive you –'

She stops abruptly, obviously remembering that Miranda's mother has just gone into a mental hospital, and Miranda, who wouldn't have dreamt of resenting the casual remark, notices her confusion and hates her for it.

Recovering quickly, Fran says, 'I wish I could make myself like it, because it's the original paper.'

A short pause. Miranda tries to think of something else to say and fails. Dad's gasping for a fag, she can tell, but Fran won't let him smoke in the house. 'Stupid little cow,' Mum said, when Miranda told her. 'That won't last.' And to show what she thought of Fran she'd lit one herself, and coughed.

Normally Miranda's good at smoothing things over. Good at hiding her feelings.

'Tea's just about ready,' Fran says. 'Nick, will you give Gareth a shout?'

Gareth's died three times in the past hour.

He can't see any way of getting through the enemy's shields without taking at least one direct hit and draining his reserves. Though if it wasn't for a certain stupid bitch who should remain nameless – *look at all that sunshine and you cooped up in here have you done your homework why don't you try reading a book for a change blah-de-blah-de-bloody blah* – he'd've wiped the buggers out long ago.

Nick puts his head round the door.

'Don't you ever knock?' Gareth asks, not taking his eyes off the screen. He has to nerve himself to say it, because Nick's sheer size sometimes frightens him. He's never hit Gareth and he never will – Mum'd go ballistic, for one thing – and yet the fear's still there. Ver-y in-ter-est-ing.

'I did, you didn't hear me. Tea's ready.'

'I don't –'

'Yes, you do. Come on, switch it off.'

'Just till the end of the game.'

'No. C'mon, Gareth, we're all waiting. Apart from anything else, it isn't very polite to your mother.'

He always says that when he means it isn't very polite to him. 'I haven't brushed my teeth.'

'You brush your teeth after meals.'

'*And* before. The main acid attack –'

Gareth can go on like this for hours. 'All right, but be quick.'

You've got to hand it to him, Nick thinks, as Gareth sidles past. It's virtually impossible to tell a child off for paying too much attention to dental hygiene. He looks round the room, thinking how typical of Gareth it is that while every other part of the house is in chaos from the move, this room is orderly. Games, neatly stacked by the computer: *Crash, Fighting Force, Mortal Kombat, Shock, Riot, Alien Trilogy, Rage, Streetfighter, Return Fire, War-hawk, Fighting Force, Nightmare Creatures, Shadowmaster, Exhumed.* In the school holidays Gareth spends, probably, forty hours a week playing these. They know they ought to stop him, and they don't, because they're only too bloody pleased to have him out of their hair. Once or twice Nick's tried, but as soon as Gareth becomes seriously upset – and of course he does, it's like taking the teat out of a baby's mouth – Fran switches sides. She'll never ever back Nick up. And he's left feeling . . . neutered. Yes, that's the right word, neutered. He's so powerless in the situation he wonders why Gareth bothers to dislike him.

Behind the locked door, Gareth starts to clean his teeth. No scrubbing up and down, no wearing away of the gums. 'Like stencilling,' the dentist says. Done properly, it takes a long time. Flossing next. And then another go with the brush at all the places where he's drawn blood.

When he's finished he spits, rinses his mouth, spits again, then turns on the tap and watches the pinky-white splats swirl away.

Lastly, he gets Nick's toothbrush from the rack, runs it several times round the lavatory bowl, under the rim where the germs lurk, inspects it for too obvious bits of shit, and restores it neatly to its place. Then, exchanging a glance with his reflection in the mirror, he dabs the last flecks of foam from his lips and goes, slowly and carefully, downstairs.

Miranda eats the burnt potatoes stoically, making no comment. Gareth spits them out. Nick takes a deep breath, opens his mouth, thinks better of it. The meal proceeds in silence except for Jasper's good-humoured babble.

'Is he talking yet?' Miranda asks.

She's only trying to make conversation, but Fran, undermined by the table manners of one son, doesn't feel like discussing the linguistic inadequacies of the other. 'Would you like baked beans instead?'

'No, he wouldn't,' Nick says. 'He can eat what he's given like everybody else.'

Fran glares at him. Why, Nick thinks, is he continually goaded into acting like Gareth's father – his 'real' father, whatever that means – and then choked off the moment he attempts it? Even when they'd gone to see the educational psychologist together he'd scarcely been allowed to say anything. He'd had to sit and listen while Fran propounded her theory that poor little Gareth was being bullied at school. Perhaps he is. But what precipitated his referral to the school psychology service was an incident in which he and another boy had upended a four-year-old and rammed his head into a lavatory bowl, which they then proceeded to flush.

Which hardly counts as *being* bullied.

You don't like him, she'd said, when Nick finally exploded.

No, I don't, he thought, looking at the gob of spat-out potato. Who could?

'Can I get down now?' Gareth asks.

'Yes, all right,' Fran sighs. 'Off you go.'

Clearing away the table a few minutes later, Nick says, 'He warmed up to Miranda, didn't he?'

'Jasper?'

'I didn't mean Gareth.'

'More than she did to him.'

'She's not used to babies.'

'Christ Almighty, Nick, will you stop defending her before she's attacked? She doesn't have to like babies. I wish I didn't.'

'You don't.'

'What?'

'Like babies. You like the idea of them.'

'Oh, very bloody clever. I just wish I wasn't too tired to appreciate it. *I* was up all night, remember?'

'Fran, what do you want me to do? I'm doing the bloody decorating –'

'Don't make it sound like a favour. You live here too, you know. And Miranda.'

'That's it, isn't it?' A pause. 'You knew I had a daughter. I took Gareth on.'

'No, you didn't. You're a lousy stepfather, you know you are.'

Nick starts to speak and checks himself. 'Well, whatever I am, at least I'm here.'

'Meaning? No, go on.'

'Doesn't matter.'

'Meaning his father wasn't?'

'Let's not have a row, Fran. Not tonight.'

'We're not having a row!'

'Well, he wasn't, was he?'

'All right, he wasn't. So what else is new?'

Nick sighs and puts his hand on the bulge. 'How's number two?'

'Three. You might at least get the number right.'

'It's going to be all right, you know. It's bound to be awful at the moment because the house is in such a mess, but it will get better.'

Made jealous by the intensity of the conversation, Jasper pushes between them, crying to be picked up. Fran bends down and lifts him into her arms. 'I'll take him up.'

'OK. I'll finish this.'

At the top of the kitchen steps she turns. 'I thought we might get a video tonight.'

'Yeah, fine. Whatever.'

Miranda curls up on the cushions, and draws the curtain half across, wishing she had a book to read, like Jane Eyre, with pictures of birds and frozen wastes, but Gran hadn't let her pack any books because they weighed a ton, she said, though Miranda carried them, she didn't. Instead she presses her face against the glass, misting it with her breath, feeling like a prisoner in a tower, but a nice feeling, not like a real prisoner – and then she remembers her last sight of Mum, standing at the end of a long corridor in the hospital, hugging herself, sunlight from the tall windows showing up all the wrinkles and grey hair.

She didn't go in voluntarily, she was 'sectioned', a horrible word that makes Miranda think of dissecting small animals.

Unable to bear thinking about it, she jumps up, and starts brushing her hair, pressing down hard till it crackles and clings to the bristles. If you do that long enough and then tear paper into tiny bits and drag your hair across it, all the bits fly upwards and stick to the ends. Angie showed her how to do it when she slept over once, and afterwards they brushed their hair in the dark and you could see the sparks. And then Angie said, 'What's wrong with your mum?' And she said, 'Nothing.' She wanted to ask, 'Why?' but didn't dare.

'Somebody's been putting green fly on my roses.' After they were sprayed the buds had millions of dead flies all over them, like caps of grey scurf.

A knock on the door. It's Gareth, blinking in that awful way of his, like a cat when it wants to be friends, though with Gareth it means the opposite.

'Come on, then,' he says.

'Come on where?'

'I've got to show you the garden.'

She starts to close the door. 'Seen it.'

'Your dad said.'

Miranda hesitates. Probably Dad had said it: he was keen on her and Gareth 'getting on'. 'All right.'

She's taller than he is, but the extra height only makes her feel exposed, like a giraffe with a pale soft belly walking with a hyena. She doesn't know how to deal with him, he's so unrelentingly horrible, all the time, and she hasn't done anything. It would be better if they just avoided each other, but Dad won't let them do that. They've got to be friends, because that makes *him* feel better.

So they go on outings. She and Gareth sitting in the back of the car, separated by Jasper, sticky, screaming, smelly Jasper, who keeps bashing them in the face with plastic toys covered in spit, and at the end of the day Fran asks in her tight voice whether they've enjoyed themselves, and Miranda says politely that she has, and Gareth says no, it was a load of crap, he'd rather have stayed at home, and the back of Dad's neck goes red.

'The garden,' Gareth says, opening the door.

The terrace, a stretch of overgrown lawn, flower beds with roses – roses everywhere – and behind them the humped dark shapes of rhododendrons.

Gareth's staring at her. 'Are you going to be here all summer?'

'I don't know.'

'Mum doesn't want you here.'

'That's all right, I don't want to *be* here.'

'So why are you?'

'My mother's ill. She's in hospital.'

'What sort of ill?'

'Depression.'

Gareth hesitates, unaware of his ground. 'You don't go into hospital with that.'

'That's all you know.'

'She's mad.'

'She isn't.'

'She's in the bin.'

'*Hospital*,' Miranda repeats steadily.

'Your dad says you're going the same way.'

'Liar.'

'He did, I heard him. He says, "I'm sometimes afraid she'll go the same way, she's such a moody child. It's not natural to be so so . . . interverted."'

'I don't believe you.'

Gareth shrugs. 'Suit yourself.'

Nick had said interverted, though not about Miranda. On one of their first trips to the Child Guidance Clinic Gareth was left alone in the playroom, while Mum and Nick and Miss Rowe went off to talk, but he wasn't having any of that. As soon as the door closed behind them he went out on to the patio, looked round to make sure he wasn't being observed, then dropped to his knees and crawled along until he was under Miss Rowe's window.

Do you think he's being bullied? Mum asked, and then Nick lost his temper and said all sorts of things. Piss-arse bastard. Shit. Gareth chipped away at the plaster underneath the windowsill, and noticed a chrysalis hanging there, as brown and dry as a dead leaf, though when he squashed it with his thumb yellowy-white stuff spurted out.

'They were in bed, talking,' he says.

They're walking across the lawn, their feet leaving silver trails in the long grass. Behind the rose bed a path starts, bordered on either side by rhododendrons. Pale green shoots of new growth thrusting through this year's dead flowers, already brown, covered with myriads of tiny insects. Miranda walks with her bare arms bunched together in front of her, not liking the sticky feel of the dead blooms on her skin.

Almost hidden by the rhododendrons is a small circular brick structure, capped by rusty iron. Gareth jumps on to it, looking down at her with narrowed eyes. 'Do you know what this is?'

Miranda shrugs.

'It's a well. A girl drowned herself in it, that's why it's covered up.' He waits for a reply. 'She used to sleep in your room.'

'Grow up, Gareth.'

'She went mad and drowned herself and nobody knew where she was till the water turned green and –'

'Nerd.'

'She walks along the corridor in the middle of the night all dripping wet and groaning and the flesh is dropping off her bones and –'

'Anorak.'

Bored with her now, he starts drifting towards the house, calling across his shoulder, ''S true.'

It isn't true, he's just saying it to frighten her. Everybody thinks old houses are haunted, but they're not, it's just rubbish. She sits down, only to jump as Gareth leaps on to the well behind her.

'She's still down there, you know.'

Miranda feels him squat behind her, his breath coming in quick excited bursts on the nape of her neck.

'They never got her out.'

When she says nothing, he straightens up, slowly, uncoiling his spine one vertebra at a time, and stands for a moment, his scuffed-toed trainers jutting out over the edge of the well, before he jumps down and walks back to the house, beating the bushes on either side with his clenched fists.

She doesn't move.

Ding dong bell
Pussy's in the well

It isn't true.

Sometimes I'm afraid she'll go the same way.

Probably Dad did say it. Gareth couldn't make that up; he can't even get 'introverted' right. She looks up at the house, working out which window's hers, whether she'll be able to see the well from her room, and closes her mind to the coming night.

THREE

Stars stream past as he soars up and away from the battle, raking the enemy ship with gunfire as he skims along its vast side. A cargo ship, slow-moving, easy prey, but then a hatch opens and dozens of one-man fighters stream out like seeds from a dandelion clock. Six lock on to him, no time to turn, he takes a blow on the shields, dives to the left, the sky tilting round him, and sees, dead ahead, five more –

He stares at the red fireball of his own death.

Think.

Rumble, rumble, clatter, broom-broom . . . Jasper zooming up and down the corridor in his car. Can't bloody think. 'Mum,' he yells, standing accusingly in the doorway. 'Does he have to make that noise? I can't concentrate.'

'Weather like this, you should be outside.'

'Why can't *he* go outside?'

'Because he's too little to go on his own and I'm changing the sheets.'

'SHURRUP!' Gareth roars at Jasper, who begins to whimper, sitting inside his red car at the other end of the corridor. 'Just shut it, will you?'

Before Fran can speak Gareth goes back into his room and slams the door. On the floor, put out for her to clear away, are two plates covered in congealed tomato sauce. My God, he must think she's running a doss house. She tries to open the door to give him a piece of her mind, but he's locked it. 'Gareth?' She bangs with her clenched fist. No answer – only the *flit-flit* of laser guns. Jasper's settled to a steady grizzle by the time she reaches him. 'Come on, let's leave him,' she says, stroking his hair. 'You've got a grumpy brother.' We've never had enough time, she thinks. Right from the beginning there's always been Gareth, as jealous of Jasper as a toddler, but without the charm that makes a toddler's jealousy acceptable.

Getting herself, the plates, the car and Jasper through two safety gates, one at the top and one at the bottom of the stairs, takes a long time – time she spends becoming very angry. It's all very well for Nick, admittedly he's got his grandfather ill, and he has to go over and see to things, she accepts that, but meanwhile she's expected to wash, iron, change sheets, cook, shop, clean – all on four hours' sleep a night. Oh, and supply conversation and entertainment – the little darlings' minds have to be stimulated. They mustn't be bored. Well – *ouch*, she thinks, snagging her varicose veins on the second safety gate – she's fucking fed up with it. If they want something to do there's a whole house full of things to do, things that desperately need doing, and they can start by decorating the living room.

She goes into the living room, to remind herself of how awful it is. God, the wallpaper's terrible. She and Nick planned to do the decorating together, after the kids were in bed, scraping away at paper when they're already tired at the end of a hard day's work. Well, no way, José. Tonight, as soon as Nick gets back from the hospital, there's going to be a decorating party. She'll get pizzas in, make it look like a treat, but in the end she's determined that just for once they're all going to behave like a proper family. It'll be fun, she tells herself, looking at the wall.

Nick opens the living-room door, sees buckets, cloths, scrapers and a stepladder. My God, she means it. A choppy sea of paint-daubed dust sheets covers the floor. Jasper's marooned behind the gauze mesh of his playpen, one cheek scarlet. Nick rests his own cheek against it as he carries him down to the kitchen. 'That rotten old tussie-peg bothering you? You're in the wars, aren't you, son?'

Like your dad. Last thing he needs after being stuck in a board meeting with a load of vacillating academics is to spend the evening decorating. Couple of stiff gins and something mindless on the box. Make sure of the gins anyway. One-handed, he opens the freezer and

31

gropes about for the ice tray. 'I can't seem to find any ice.'

Fran's voice from along the corridor. 'Try harder, darling.'

There isn't any, beloved. Back across the floor, picking his way between red, yellow, blue and orange men wielding the tools of their various trades – full employment in the plastic world anyway – he opens the fridge door. No lemons. Ah well. Dragging Jasper's toy box into the middle of the floor, he begins sweeping up workmen with dustpan and brush and throwing them into the box. Jasper screams with rage and takes them out again. 'Don't do that, Jasper,' Nick says, uncoiling his son's sticky fingers from an orange plumber.

Jasper screams again, louder, bringing Fran down the stairs, open-armed and indignant. 'Do you have to do that, Nick? There must be a better way.'

Nick swigs his ice-less, lemon-less gin. Fran heaves one huge breast out of her sweatshirt and plugs the howling child on to it. There's something disturbing about his broad sticky hand kneading Fran's breast. High time he was weaned, it isn't good for her. The drained face, the straggly hair, the huge belly, the skinny, sharp-boned cat-with-too-many-litters look, it reminds Nick of some awful Victorian pamphlet advocating the virtues of self-restraint. Not that he's exactly tempted to abandon it. The truth is he's repelled by her, but the truth frightens him and he sheers away from it. Jasper stares at him accusingly round the curve of his mother's breast. 'Sorry,' Nick says, sitting down and immediately leaping up again. 'What on earth is that?'

'He was sick,' says Fran distantly. 'I've been meaning to clear it up.'

Miranda comes into the kitchen in time to see Nick drop his trousers. 'Can I help?' she asks, looking from Fran's breasts to Dad's Thing and rapidly down at the floor.

'Throw it out,' Fran said.

Miranda stares at her.

'The cushion. I'm not washing it.'

Miranda picks up the cushion fastidiously between thumb and forefinger, and takes it outside.

Silence. Nick says, 'I better phone in the order if we're having pizzas.'

'All right.'

She sounds indifferent, her attention focused entirely on Jasper. Look at me, Nick wants to say. Instead he goes to the bottom of the stairs and calls Gareth, who for once appears without having to be threatened or cajoled. Perhaps he's hungry. Or perhaps he senses there's something going on.

Nick rings in the order. He has to repeat the address.

'That's not the Summerfield estate, is it?'

'No.'

'Only we don't deliver there.'

'How long will you be?'

'Half an hour.'

'Half an hour,' Nick repeats, replacing the receiver.

'Believe that, you'll believe anything,' says Gareth. 'They'll get lost.'

'No, they won't. But I think we might as well get started, don't you?'

Nick and Fran look at each other.

'Right. I'll see you in there,' she says.

In the living room, Nick and Miranda pick up their scrapers in silence. Barbara's moods had brought them closer together. Fran's can't be mentioned.

After a while Nick asks, 'Where's Gareth?'

'I don't know.'

He goes to the door. 'Where's Gareth?'

Fran hands Jasper over. 'I'm on my way.'

Shouts from upstairs, then Gareth appears, looking shocked. 'Mum switched my computer off.'

'Don't worry,' says Nick. 'It's not a life-support machine.'

Gareth looks at the buckets. 'Do we have to?'

'Yes,' says Fran.

'Why can't we decorate our own rooms?'

'Because we're a family,' Nick says. 'And this is *our* room.'

Jasper, arms on the rails of his playpen, nappy sagging between his knees, swigging orange juice from his bottle, looks like a bucolic and disreputable Farmer Giles. Peal after peal of laughter greets the children's efforts to splash wallpaper remover on to the walls without getting it in their eyes, and when Gareth trips over a bucket and falls headlong Jasper chuckles round the teat till he nearly chokes.

'Oh, very bloody funny,' Gareth says.

The wallpaper darkens under their cloths. At first Nick tries to talk, but then, when there's no response, turns on the radio.

'Christ,' Gareth says.

'Choose what you want, then.'

Gareth fiddles with the knobs, producing a blare of sound that makes conversation impossible. They scrape away, the paper coming off inch by painful inch. Half an hour passes, then a further ten minutes.

'Told you they'd get lost,' Gareth says.

Jasper's getting tired. He pulls at his ears, dribbles and wails until eventually Fran picks him up and sniffs his crotch. 'I think he needs changing.'

'Can we change him for one that doesn't scream?' Gareth asks.

The nappy's full and pungent. Fran presses her hand hard into the small of her back, as she kneels down.

'You sit down,' Nick says. 'I'll do it.'

Fran won't use disposable nappies, because of the rain forests or blue algae or something. Normally Nick's a dab hand with squares of cotton and Velcro, but tonight he's tired, and suddenly Jasper seems to have six heels and shit on every single one of them. Not solid either –

a paste that spreads relentlessly from bottom to feet to hands to oh my *God* his mouth.

Very distinctly, as if giving lessons in elocution, Fran says, 'Nick, you are without doubt the most completely useless man it has ever been my misfortune to meet.'

Nick throws down the nappy, and walks off.

'Would you pass the baby wipes, Miranda?' Fran asks.

Miranda hands her the box, and in the process gets a closer look at Jasper. 'Ugh. Oh dear.' She swallows hard. 'Would you mind if I sat down?'

'What's wrong with *you*?' Fran asks.

'"I think I'm going to faint,"' warbles Gareth.

'Nothing.'

'Is it your period?'

'*No*,' says Miranda, with an agonized glance at Gareth. 'I'm just tired. I didn't sleep very well.'

'She's afraid of ghosts,' says Gareth.

'I'm *not*.'

'There aren't any ghosts,' says Nick sharply.

'There aren't any pizzas either.'

Nick draws a deep breath. 'I'll ring.'

In the hall he stands for a moment, gazing up into the darkness at the top of the stairs. He didn't like that remark of Gareth's about Miranda being afraid of ghosts. Gareth's capable of playing some very cruel games, but there's nothing he can do about that at the moment. Pizzas, he thinks, and reaches for the phone.

A brief, acrimonious conversation, then he bangs the

36

phone down and goes back into the living room. 'Another ten minutes.'

'Ssh,' says Fran, who's trying to get Jasper off to sleep.

Miranda's picked up her scraper again.

'Sure you're all right?' Nick asks.

'Fine.'

They must have been working in total silence for five minutes when Gareth says, 'I've found a foot.'

'What?' Nick asks.

'A foot. Drawing of.'

'Can't be.' Nick bends down, and scrapes away another inch of paper. 'Do you know, I think he's right?'

'Thank you.'

'I wonder if there's any more?'

Miranda forgets about feeling ill. Everybody forgets about the pizzas. They angle the lamps more closely and start scraping again, revealing a whole shoe, the draping of cloth across a flexed knee, a hand clasping the arm of a chair.

Once he's got an idea of the scale, Nick splashes stripper on to the wall where he thinks the head must be, becoming more excited as he works, for what's emerging is no stick drawing, no crude approximation of a man, but a strongly individual face. The eyes keenly alert, he seems to lean out of the wall. A glitter of intelligence, almost too keen, rapacious even. Instinctively, Nick looks to the mouth for confirmation, but the walrus moustache, drooping over the upper lip, makes its expression difficult to read.

Ruthless, perhaps? At any rate, the impression is one of power.

'Fanshawe,' Nick says. 'Has to be.'

'The clothes are right,' says Fran, coming to stand beside him. 'I mean, he looks Victorian.'

Just behind Fanshawe's shoulder is a button belonging to somebody else's jacket. A toddler's dimpled fist rests on his left knee.

'It's a family portrait,' Nick says slowly.

The doorbell chimes. Fran goes to answer it and comes back carrying a stack of white cartons. 'Pizzas.'

They break off and eat, gazing all the time at the wall. Miranda's whiter than ever, but when Nick asks if she wants to lie down she simply shakes her head. Fran's got two distinct spots of colour in her cheeks. Nick can hardly force the food down, though he makes himself eat two slices before he gives up. Gareth goes back to the wall, leaving his pizza uneaten. A second later Miranda follows him.

'I'll start over there,' Fran says. 'I think we should spread out.'

Wiping sweat from his upper lip, Nick says, 'Let's have a window open, shall we? Gareth?'

They've kept the windows closed, in spite of the heat, because there are no curtains. Gareth sees his own white face reflected in the window, surrounded by clouds of pale moths with fat furry bodies fumbling at the glass, trying to get in. As soon as he opens it they flicker past him, and begin dancing round the lamps. One finds its way on to the hot bulb and dies in a sizzle of scorched wings.

Gradually, the portrait's revealed. A red-haired woman emerges from under Fran's scraper, with the sour expression of someone who's driven a hard bargain and is not contented with the result. Behind her stands a girl with thin ringlets dangling round a frail-looking neck. Huge eyes – her father's eyes – the underlids so prominent it's like one of those trick drawings where the face still looks normal upside-down. This effect isn't, as it would be on most young faces, pathetic, but faintly sinister.

Behind Fanshawe stands a boy, slightly taller than the girl. Dark eyes, a strained expression that Nick recognizes, yet can't identify. One hand rests on his father's shoulder, though only because he's been told to put it there. His fingertips cringe from the enforced contact. The boy painted this: there's no way of proving it, but Nick knows. That expression is the inward-directed gaze of the self-portraitist. And my God, what a talent. The faces leap out of the wall.

Nick begins working his way down over Fanshawe's waistcoat, leaning over Miranda, who's kneeling between his feet.

'Oh, look –' she says.

'What is it?'

'I don't know.'

He can hear in her voice that she does. He bends down

and peers into the space she's created. An erect penis springs from the unbuttoned flies, as thick and pale as the decaying cabbage stalks in the kitchen garden. Gareth looks across and sniggers.

'Well,' says Nick.

Fran says, 'It's horrible.'

'Oh, I don't know . . . '

'No, I mean the whole thing's horrible.'

Nick's begun to feel that too. His early excitement's giving way to dismay, as it becomes clearer, minute by minute, that the portrait's an exercise in hate.

Gareth's scraping away at the bodice of the seated woman. 'Boobs,' he announces triumphantly.

The woman's breasts are great lard-white footballs, covered by a canal system of blue veins.

Fran winces. 'I wonder what other surprises he's got in store?'

At the centre of the group, uncovered last, is a small, fair-haired boy, whose outstretched arms, one podgy fist resting on the knee of either parent, forms the base-line of the composition. Patches of wallpaper still cling to the painting like scabs of chicken pox, but even so its power is clear. Victorian paterfamilias, wife and children: two sons, a daughter. Pinned out, exhibited. Even without the exposed penis, the meticulously delineated and hated breasts, you'd have sensed the tension in this family, with the golden-haired toddler at its dark centre.

Their shadows half obscure the figures on the wall.

'Come back behind the lamps,' Nick says.

They move back, until only the flickering moths move across the surface, casting shadows as big as birds.

'Who do you suppose did it?' Fran asks.

'The boy,' says Nick.

'It could've been one of the workmen,' Fran says, sounding defensive. But why defensive? 'I don't suppose they'd be doing their own decorating.'

'No, it's the boy,' Nick insists. 'Look at his eyes. He's the only one who knows he's in a painting.'

Fran stares from face to face. 'Yes,' she says at last.

Silence. The living stand and gaze at the dead. Probably the same thought occurs to all of them, but it's Miranda, her voice edging up into hysteria, who finally says what they're all thinking. 'It's us.'

Nick opens his mouth to contradict her, but no words come out.

'No, it isn't,' Fran says gratingly, in a voice she scarcely recognizes as hers. '*She's* not pregnant.'

FOUR

Upstairs Fran drops a nightdress over her head, and takes off her bra and pants under the cover of its folds. She doesn't want Nick to see her naked, can't bear her reflection in the mirror even, and all because of that obscene thing downstairs. She saw how Gareth stared at the breasts and then at her. The penis wasn't so bad somehow. There was nothing satyr-like about it, nothing comic or sensual or friendly. Phallus as weapon, pure and simple, but she didn't think Nick had felt attacked by the portrait. Not the way she had. She'd been wounded by those breasts.

She lies on the edge of the bed, her hands cradling the bag of drowning kittens her stomach's become. 'We've got to cover that thing up.'

'Can't be tomorrow. I've got to see Geordie.'

'Can't you leave it another day?'

'No, he'll be conscious tomorrow.'

Silence. He waits for her to try again.

'Did you see how upset Miranda was?'

Yes, he'd also seen how upset Fran was. He gets into

bed and touches her shoulder. 'We could have a cuddle.'

'I'm too tired. Sorry.'

A pause. 'All right.' He turns away and lies on his back in the darkness. 'I did mean a cuddle.'

No reply. After a few minutes he can tell from her breathing that she's asleep.

Monday he'll start getting the rest of the paper off. Make that the first job. Fran's right, it can't be left like that, but tomorrow he has to see Geordie.

His hands throb. The extraordinary thing is that although every inch of the paper had been a struggle to remove — and he has blisters on the palms of his hands to prove it — his last impression, before he drifts off to sleep, is that the portrait had risen to the surface of its own volition, that it would have been impossible to keep it hidden any longer, rather as a mass of rotting vegetation, long submerged, will rise suddenly to the surface of a pond.

Miranda waits for the house to be quiet before she gets out of bed. Her room's dark, because it overlooks the back garden, darker than her bedroom at home, which has a street lamp outside. Thick velvety black that threatens to suffocate her. Every night she lies awake, waiting for the girl to come in, knowing all the time she won't, and yet waiting anyway.

Only now the girl has a face. She has to see her again. She slips her hand into the drawer of the bedside table and finds the torch. She's not sure it makes things better, because everything outside the wobbling circle of light becomes blacker, but she needs it to find her way downstairs.

On the landing she listens. Dad snoring, bed springs creaking, no sound from Jasper's room, a constant *flit-flit* from Gareth's, which means he's on the computer again. She starts to walk downstairs, eyes lowered, looking at nothing but her feet, which become more and more weird as she watches them, like small nocturnal animals creeping about.

The door to the living room's closed. She switches off the torch before she opens it, in case the light could be seen from the road. Somebody might think the house is being burgled. Moonlight, reflected from the daubed white sheets that cover the floor, gives enough light to move around by, though she sees the figures in the painting only as patches of darkness against the pale plaster.

Close to the wall she switches the torch on again, and instantly, like the pupil of an eye contracting, the room recedes. Now there's only the faces and her fingers on the torch.

One after another the point of light summons them back from the dark. The father, the mother, the elder brother and the little boy. She leaves the girl till last, because she's the one Miranda dreads seeing most. When at last she shines the torch into those eyes, she notices that the minute cracks in the plaster look like lines in the iris.

The room's cold. She backs away from the portrait – it's too powerful a presence for her to feel comfortable with it behind her. Only at the last moment can she bring herself to look away, pulling the door closed as quietly as somebody leaving a sick room.

In the room that has always been the nursery, Jasper sleeps in the cot he's almost outgrown. His hands, raised on either side of his head, are curled like new fern fronds. A cloud begins to drift across the moon, a shadow encroaches on the pillow, and Jasper whimpers as it passes over his face.

The moon sails clear. White light falls on the choppy sea of dust sheets covering the living-room floor. The Fanshawes, visible again, though now there's no one to see them, gaze through the french windows over the lawns, the rose beds, and the rhododendron bushes of the garden that had once been theirs.

FIVE

Slim and sexy, Queen Victoria gazes out from her plinth to where the wrinkled Tyne crawls beneath its six bridges. Above her head seagulls squeal like abandoned puppies.

Craning his head back to see her face, Nick realizes again how long his grandfather's life has been. This Victoria, broader in the beam but awesomely stable, still sat on the throne when Grandad took his first steps. Now, inside the hospital named after her, older than Victoria on her deathbed, older than most of us will ever be, Geordie sits on a plastic chair beside the window and looks out at a few blowzy roses dropping their petals on to the wet soil.

The last rose of summer, Nick thinks, left blooming alone, though blooming's hardly the right word. He's wearing a white gown, the kind that slips on at the front and ties at the back. They've wedged a white cellular blanket between his back and the chair, because he's already showing signs of bedsores.

It's unusual to find him alone like this. Usually he's one

of the few old men on the ward who's found somebody to talk to, grumble to rather, complaining he misses his midday pint, he's all bunged up with that stuff they gave him for the X-rays, he's dying for a fag. Grousing – an old soldier's version of stoicism. He's a health educationalist's nightmare. He's had his telegram from the Queen, framed it, hung it over the mantelpiece. Cigarettes have never hurt *him*, he says, and what's more there's nothing beats a Woodbine for bursting lice eggs in the seams of your shirt – though at this point the person he's talking to generally starts to edge away.

'Hello, Grandad,' Nick says, putting a bunch of green grapes on the table beside the bed.

Geordie looks at the grapes with suspicion, thinking the pips will insinuate themselves between his dentures and his gums, and wreak havoc.

'Seedless. How are you?'

'Middling.'

'Fair to middling?'

'No, if you must know, middling to bloody awful.'

Nick sits on the end of the bed. 'Is this the first time you've been out of bed?'

'No, they had me up for an hour last night.'

His cheeks are furrowed over naked gums, the neck protruding from the gown is thin and scaly, there's several days' growth of beard on his chin, but he doesn't look inconsiderable or pathetic. He looks like Caravaggio's portrait of St Jerome.

'They haven't shaved you, then?'

'They offered. I can't stand the chewing.'

'Might make you feel better.'

'It's all very well for you,' Geordie flashes back. 'You don't have to cope with young bits of lasses shoving their fingers up your arse every verse end.'

'They are doctors, Grandad.'

'Aye' – doubtfully.

He looks so lost that Nick impulsively bends down and hugs him: a brief embarrassed collision of rough chins that has Geordie pulling away at once. It's not rejection. It's just that nothing must be allowed to disturb his position, which is very finely calculated to keep the pain asleep.

'Bloody torture, this is,' he says, grunting, after Nick's straightened up.

'Pain? You should –'

'Ask them for more of yon stuff? I will not. I don't know where I am with it.'

They sit in silence for a moment.

'Anyway, I didn't mean that. I meant the fags. Do you know I have to walk all the way down that corridor if I want a fag? Can't smoke in here. I says, "Can't I nip out the french windows and have one?" *No.* Anyway if I stand up I show me arse. Have you seen this?'

He pulls at the shift to show the string fastenings at the back and the movement wakes up the pain. For a moment he says nothing at all – just fights it silently.

When it seems to have died down a bit, Nick asks gently, 'Does it matter?'

''Course it bloody matters. See that lad over there?' He's pointing at one of the nurses. 'Ian. Nice lad and all that but a nance if ever I saw one.'

The nice lad's dispensing lunch from a trolley.

'Are you allowed to eat now?'

'Allowed yes. Whether I can's another matter.'

He seems entirely clear mentally, better than he was before he went into hospital, though his bearing's not as erect as it normally is.

'Are the stitches starting to pull?'

'They are a bit.'

'Do you mind if I have a look?'

Using the white blanket as a screen, Geordie pulls up his shift to reveal the red centipede crawling up his stomach, past that other scar, the one he brought back with him from France.

'It's healing well,' Nick says.

Geordie's penis, retracted into the brown rugosities of his scrotum, looks like a rose in a bed of dead leaves.

'Itching's supposed to be a good sign, isn't it?'

'Yes, I think it is.'

Nick wonders how much Geordie understands. How much he minds. Other people don't respond to this illness as they normally would. They say things like: 'Oh, well, he's had a good innings,' as if so many years of cheating death must automatically mean he's reconciled to it now.

49

But is he? Perhaps he's as rebellious and afraid as Nick himself would be? He's had so much longer than most people can hope for – he's almost not allowed to want to live.

'You sleeping all right?'

'Not bad.'

He's looking along the ward now, watching Ian's slow progress from bed to bed. Despite saying he can't eat, he's looking forward to his lunch, though perhaps only because mealtimes give shape to the endless amorphous hospital days.

Ian reaches the bed. He's a pink-skinned plump lad with fair wavy hair and a buoyant manner. 'Do you want it there, Mr Lucas, or would you rather have it in bed?'

Seeing his chance, Geordie says, 'Bed. I can't manage it here.'

Ian on one side, Nick on the other, they lift him as gently as they can and yet he's hurt badly, biting his lip, grunting, finally letting his head fall back against the pillows. They leave him for a while, then straighten his legs out.

Ian hesitates, looking at the five beds he still has to do.

'Put it on the table,' Nick says. 'I'll help him.'

It's a few minutes before Geordie can take any interest in food at all, and when he tastes it he's not thrilled. 'Iron filings,' he says, not grumbling, he knows perfectly well the taste's in his mouth.

'Try to eat a bit.'

Nick watches him chew, thinking that any nourishment now can only prolong the agony and that perhaps he ought to be encouraging him not to eat. He thinks of Paul Morel diluting his mother's milk so that it won't nourish her. Finally poisoning her, partly in compassion, partly in unconscious revenge because her milk had poisoned him. And that sets off another train of thought about ambivalent relationships and the dangers of euthanasia. Then he realizes what he's thinking and drags his thoughts back to the ward. It seems unforgivable, when there's so little time left, to wander off like that.

Geordie's getting tired. Nick takes over, spooning mashed potato and gravy into the toothless mouth. Sometimes the pap's regurgitated, and has to be caught on the spoon and reinserted. It's like feeding Jasper; he's an expert. He gets half a dozen spoonfuls in before Geordie waves him almost angrily away. 'That'll do,' he says.

Nick pushes the wheeled table to the foot of his bed and settles him back more comfortably on the pillows. 'Tea?'

'Aye, go on.'

Nick tips the beaker and a little dribbles into Geordie's mouth. He watches the bulbous Adam's apple jerking as he drinks.

'That's enough, son.'

Son, Nick thinks. Yes. Fair enough.

★

When Nick was growing up Grandad's silent presence in the house had been only one more oddity in the way their lives were lived.

Nick's father was the Headmaster of a small preparatory school; his mother was the Matron. As a small boy he was always aware of another world on the other side of the door in the hall, though until he was seven he was forbidden to enter the school.

Every Sunday, in term, half a dozen boys would come to tea, sitting out on the lawn in summer on their best behaviour, making polite conversation in high-pitched self-confident voices. Once when Nick was almost seven one of the boys met him accidentally in the hall and gave him a Chinese burn. Not for any reason. He just did. Nick's eyes watered. 'Don't tell,' the boy said, going out on to the lawn. Nick stared at the red marks left by his fingers and pulled his sleeve down to hide them. Then he went and sat at the table and watched the boy's mouth moving delicately up and down as he chewed a piece of cake. He didn't say anything, and when Mummy came in to say goodnight he didn't say anything then either. He lay in the dark, not bothering to wonder why the boy had done it. It was just something that happened. He hadn't known that before, but he recognized it now.

When he was seven he went through the door in the hall and into his father's school and the door closed quietly behind him, with a small puff of sound.

The two worlds smelled different: furniture polish,

Mummy's scent, good cooking, clean carpets one side of the door; custard, boiled cabbage, gym shoes, Jeyes fluid, grey wool, small-boy smell on the other. His father, who was immensely tall and towered over the bed when he came upstairs to say goodnight, became an even taller man on a platform saying prayers. When you met him in the corridors you had to remember to call him Sir. For the first few weeks he was 'Da-Sir', but Nick learned quickly. He had to. 'Mummy' was more difficult because it started with the same letter as Matron. He never called her Mummy at school, but he often called her Matron at home, once at a family tea party and all the aunts and uncles laughed. Nick didn't think it was funny. (Forty years on, with children of his own, he knows it wasn't funny.)

Life was full of traps. Nick's father had the essential apparatus of a good disciplinarian: eyes in his arse. He knew about the smoking in the copse behind the school, he knew which boys slipped out between prep and dinner to lay bets at the local betting shop, he knew who was being bullied and who was doing it, just knew, but the boys didn't believe that. Nick was always suspected of telling tales, though he said nothing, clammed up about school as soon as he was safely on the other side of the door. All the temptations to betray were the other way round.

Very few boys were prepared to risk the charge of 'sucking up' by becoming his friend, and he was desperate to belong. Once, when he was eleven, they were all talking about sex. Did the Queen and the Duke of Edinburgh do it? No, they unanimously decided. The Vicar and his wife? No. Mr Halford and Matron? Sidelong glances at Nick, giggles.

'Yes,' he said. 'I heard them.'

Later, one of the boys, the one he most wanted to have as a friend, said, 'You shouldn't have said that.'

Nick became a spectacularly devious child. Every second of every day was supervised by Da-Sir or Mu-Matron; the only privacy was inside his head. He lied automatically all the time about everything. Once when he was a teenager his mother came into his bedroom and asked him what he was reading. *Kidnapped*, he said, quick as a flash, pushing *Treasure Island* out of sight under his pillow. But lying, he soon realized, wasn't enough. However good you were, you made mistakes. You had to be two people, one in each world, and in each world you had to forget the responses of the other.

Only Grandad, silent, wreathed in blue cigarette smoke, never changed; belonged only to one world.

His face, yellow against the white cloth of the pillows, doesn't change much now either, though fugitive expressions pass across it rather like the mouthings of newborn babies, reactions generally to what's going on in their guts. His are like that too, his whole attention focused inwards on managing the pain. A white line runs from his temple to the centre of his cheek, an old wound, as much a part of him now as the colour of his eyes. It's difficult to believe he wasn't born with it, though he'd lived the first eighteen years of his life without it. Another inch to the left and it would have taken out the eye.

Nick wonders whether he should go now, or at least walk along to the visitors' café and have a cup of coffee, give Grandad a break, but he no sooner stands up with this in mind than Grandad says, 'Don't go.' It's the first sign he's shown in the last ten minutes that he's aware of Nick's presence.

'Where's the pain?' Nick says.

'Down there. Like always wanting to shit.'

'Do they give you injections?'

'Just pills.' He rouses himself slightly. 'Do you know they shaved me legs as well?' He hoists himself up the bed. 'I says, "What you shaving them for?" It was Ian. He says, "Don't blame me. Sister's a navel-to-knee woman. You lose your bush round here if you're having your tonsils out."'

The groin is hairless, infantile. He doesn't seem to mind, but perhaps he does, it's difficult to tell.

'That bloody grub's on its way through,' he says.

'Do you want the bedpan?' Nick looks around for the bell.

'No, I bloody don't, I've had enough of that. How can anybody shit lying on their back?'

'You're not on your back.'

55

'Good as. I'll go to the toilet.'

He looks daunted, though, even as he says it. For so many years now there's been something almost miraculous about his body, the erect carriage – he has no arthritis – none – the eyes that still see, perfectly, the ears that still hear, perfectly – all this combined with an almost transparent thinness, a lightness, as if the next puff of wind would blow him away. He has seemed to be as fragile and indestructible as thistledown.

They make the journey to the bathroom in slow stages. So much effort to get to the side of the bed, so much to push the red, shiny, scaly legs and feet into the slippers which Nick places ready for him. Then a rest before the slow shuffle along the ward, Nick at his rear bunching up the smock behind him like a bridesmaid holding up the bride's train, concealing Grandad's lean and pleated arse from the gaze of passing nancies. Ian in particular, though Ian rubs surgical spirit into it twice a day and hasn't been carried away by passion yet.

At last they make it to the loo. A cool gush of water from the next cubicle as Nick lowers Geordie on to the seat and retreats a few tactful steps to the standups, where he pees and then stares at himself in the mirror, listening to the grunts of effort and pain from the cubicle behind him.

Another mirror, this time belonging to Grandad, a looking-glass made of steel, a hole punched through one end with a length of khaki ribbon threaded through. It hung on a hook in the corner of the bathroom where he kept his shaving things. Whenever Nick asked, Geordie took it down and let him look into it, but the reflection that peered back at him was blurry, swollen, distorted by the irregularities in the metal, never the clear reflection you got in glass. Only it didn't break. Grandad dropped it on the floor once, to show that it didn't break.

The mirror had gone with him through France, but it couldn't have been sentiment that bound him to it, for he avoided everything else to do with the war. Never spoke of it. Would walk a mile out of his way to avoid passing the war memorial. And yet every morning of his life he shaved using that mirror, the same he'd propped up against sandbags in France, had brought back across the Channel when he was wounded and taken out with him again. He would watch Nick looking at himself. 'It's funny, Grandad,' Nick would say, pulling faces to distort his reflection still further. Geordie said nothing, just waited patiently, and then when Nick had finished hung the mirror back on the hook.

He said very little. With Nick's father he was deferential in that curiously English way, though Nick sensed that beneath the surface respect there was a certain degree of contempt. 'A man among boys, a boy among men.' Whether Geordie knew the phrase or not, that had been his verdict. Though at the same time he was pleased that his Mollie, by marrying a schoolmaster, had taken several crucial steps up in the world. He was careful to mind his p's and q's whenever his son-in-law was around. Literally. He was uncomfortable with his own way of speaking, the local accent, the stammer, his inability to articulate. The stammer was bad in those years. There were times when he seemed to be hoiking up words like phlegm, raking them out of his gut.

But the silence went deeper than that. His body, stripped off in the garden – the wound in his side – suggested questions. Why? How? What happened? Nick would ask, but there were no answers. The past was hidden, veiled in silence, like his grandfather's head behind its screen of cigarette smoke.

'You know it's cancer?'

'Yes. Dr Morton told me.'

Neil Shepherd's in his early fifties. His face is grey in the grey light falling through the tall windows to the right of his desk. The growling and gurgling from the pipes that run along the wall behind him suggest ominous possibilities, but not as ominous as the state of Geordie's intestines.

'I'm afraid it's spread beyond the stomach. It wouldn't be operable even in a much younger man. I'm sorry.'

'Yes,' Nick says. 'That's more or less what I expected.'

A pause. 'How would you describe his state of mind?'

'Seems fairly cheerful.'

'Clear, mentally?'

'Why do you ask?'

'He said something the other day that seemed to imply he thought the pain was coming from his bayonet wound.'

'He's said that to me too.'

'But he must know it isn't true.'

Nick hesitates. 'When he came back from the war they had a memorial service for his brother, who was killed. And as they were leaving the church his mother, my great-grandmother, turned to him and said, "It should have been you."' He sees Shepherd wince. 'I think he needs to believe it's the bayonet wound that's killing him. I don't pretend to understand it, but I don't think it's just confusion or ignorance. He wants to believe it.'

'Even after all this time?'

Nick pulls a face. 'He seems to be getting closer to it, if anything. The nightmares are back.'

'Yes, he's very restless at night. Are you sure Mrs – I'm sorry, I've forgotten her name.'

'Mrs Wilson. His daughter. My aunt.'

'Do you think she can cope?'

'Well, she won't be coping on her own. I don't think there's any question of putting him in a home.' He pauses. 'How long do –'

Shepherd's already shaking his head. 'It really is impossible to say.'

'Educated guess?'

Another shake of the head. 'A few months, at most. Frankly, he could go any time.'

Well, yes, Nick thinks, going back to the ward, but at the age of 101 that's true even without the cancer.

Auntie Frieda's by the bed when he gets back, sitting in the plastic chair, nursing her handbag as if she suspects somebody of planning to steal it, and running her tongue round the front of her dentures as if she thinks they might have a crack at those as well. She looks disgruntled and virtuous and mildly critical, darting fierce little assessing glances round the ward.

Nick bends down and kisses her cheek, feeling how much more loosely the skin hangs from the bone than it did even a week ago. She should be resting, trying to get her strength back after the last two months of virtually round-the-clock care. Shepherd's right. She can't possibly cope on her own. 'How are you?'

'Oh, not so bad.'

Her eyes are red-rimmed, from crying perhaps. She nods at the bed curtains. 'I was just saying to your grandad, I don't dislike that shade of beige.'

Nick turns aside to hide his amusement. Auntie Frieda's enthusiasms are always couched in these negative terms: 'I wouldn't mind . . . ' 'I don't dislike . . . ' 'I can't say I object . . . ' He sometimes wonders whether her marriage remained childless because Uncle Wilf never felt sufficiently encouraged to persevere.

Grandad's back on the bed, scaly red shins peeping from below the hem of the smock.

'I'm dying for a fag,' he says, unconsciously echoing the government's latest anti-smoking campaign. 'It's bloody torture, this is.' He sets up a great grumble about the hospital's no-smoking policy, designed, Nick suspects, to deter him from too great frankness about whatever the doctor might have said. His clever grandson's talked to the doctor and sorted things out and he doesn't want to know about it, thank you very much – that seems to be the message.

'You could go to the day room if you leant on me,' Nick says.

He sees Geordie weighing the pain of the long journey against the delights of a cigarette when he gets there. 'Aye, howay.'

'I don't know,' Auntie Frieda says. 'You're as bad as each other. You egg each other on.'

This is said in her 'all men are children really' tone. Nick can see Geordie being exasperated by it, but also, secretly, liking it – as he does himself.

'I'm on if you are,' Nick says.

The old man might have changed his mind after the pain of standing upright, but he grits his teeth and hangs on. Leaning heavily on Nick, shuffling along in his scuffed slippers, gasping for breath, he's made it down the corridor, Frieda bringing up the rear with a blanket for him to sit on, and the longed-for cigarettes.

They sit at a little table with a heaped-up ash tray. A quiz show's playing on television, blurred contestants against an improbably orange backdrop, but the day room's empty except for a woman in a pink quilted dressing-gown with a shaved patch on her head, who sits at another table chain-smoking and staring blank-eyed at the screen.

'Are you going to have one?' Geordie asks Nick.

'Yeah, I'll join you,' Nick says.

Geordie lights up, closing his eyes as he inhales. 'Puts me back behind the bike shed, this does. Do you know I've gone a bit dizzy?'

A disgusted *tsk* from Frieda.

'So what did he have to say, then?' Grandad asks, fortified by his second drag.

'Not a lot.' Nick's feeling his way.

'Did he say when I can go home?'

'No.'

Nick hears Auntie Frieda's caught-in sigh of relief. She can't cope, he thinks again. It's asking too much. Grandad thinks of her as a young woman still. She's his daughter, after all – how can she not be young? He doesn't seem to see the reality of a woman in her seventies in failing health.

'Did he mention the bayonet wound?' Geordie asks.

'He did, yes, well he mentioned it.'

'I told him that's what it was,' he says, turning to Frieda, triumphant. 'I said that's what it was, didn't I?'

What's it all about, Nick wonders. The wound's given him no trouble for *eighty* years, why on earth should he

62

suppose it's started playing up now? But it's not just the wound that's moved into the forefront of his mind. For years he's been free of nightmares, flashbacks, hallucinations, all the dreadful baggage he brought back with him from France, yet in the last few months they've returned. His nights, recently, have been terrible to endure. Terrible to witness. Worse than that, he's actually become quite dangerous. Auntie Frieda's been mistaken for a German soldier more than once.

Geordie's finding the hard seat and the upright posture more and more uncomfortable. He drags impatiently at his second cigarette, no longer enjoying it, just stocking up for the famine ahead.

'That's enough,' Frieda says. 'It's time you were back in bed.'

He doesn't argue, but stands up at once.

'Are you coming back later?' he asks Frieda, on their slow progress back to the ward.

'Not tonight,' Nick says, before she can answer. 'I'll look in again before I go.'

They get him back into bed and settled under the sheet. He eases himself right down, his sparse grey hair rucked up by the pillows, and lies flat at last. His hands flap like fish along the counterpane, unhappy with the hospital tightness of the sheets around him. He wants to pull the eiderdown up to his chin, and burrow down into the warmth the way he does at home. 'Dress rehearsal for a bloody coffin,' he complains.

'Why don't you try to sleep?' Nick says, bending down to give him a hug.

The pale blue eyes fasten on his face. He's disconcerted by their sharpness, their awareness of the unintended irony of his suggestion.

'I'll sleep soon enough.'

When they reach the end of the ward and turn to look back, he lifts his hand in a gesture that's almost more a salute than a wave.

SIX

'Trouble is, he thinks I should be there all the time,' Frieda says, as they walk back to the car. 'I don't think he realizes what an awkward journey it is. I have to change buses twice.'

She's enjoying her grumble, but Nick knows he mustn't make the mistake of agreeing with her, because that will put her back into defensive mode. The wheel's turned full circle. Grandad's her baby now.

He unlocks the car door on her side, and sees her seat belt fastened before he turns the key in the ignition. There's a smell of wood smoke in the air. Autumn with its pre-packaged nostalgia is just around the corner. He feels a passionate desire to cling on to the last of the summer. He won't spend tomorrow covering up the wall painting, he decides; he'll take Fran and the kids out somewhere instead, and then finds himself yawning. He feels too tired to concentrate on anything.

'Perhaps if you told him what time to expect you? Then he'll know how long he's got to wait.'

'Hm,' Frieda says, unconvinced. She doesn't want to be rescued. But she can relax in the car, doesn't have to wait at that draughty bus shelter they're just passing, full of women like herself with pinched faces, belts knotted tightly round non-existent waists, clutching plastic bags full of dirty nightdresses and pyjamas, looking up the road for a bus that doesn't come.

'You look tired,' Nick says.

'I haven't been sleeping. Can't sleep. When I was up and down to him all the time I used to think, Oh, if only I could have a good night's sleep, but you see, I'm still listening for him. I was convinced last night I heard him get up and go out.'

Grandad's taken to wandering. Or going out on patrol. One or the other.

The car heater's making Nick drowsy. He opens the window on his side and a few spots of cold rain blow on to his face.

'You know that thing they've got him in?'

'What thing?'

'You know, the white thing.'

'The smock?'

'Yes. Do they put you in that if they know you're not going to get better?'

'No, I don't think so. It just makes bathing them easier. They don't have to pull them about so much.'

'Only I thought it might be easier for them to lay you out.'

She knows it's cancer, but she belongs to a generation that can hardly bring itself to say the word. 'The big C' was as far as he'd ever heard her go to naming it, and that was explaining the death of a woman at the bottom of the street, a woman she hardly knew. How many of the reassuring things she says to Grandad does she believe herself, and does he believe them? Is anybody saying what they think? When he next looks at her she's fallen asleep, hanging from the seat belt like a toddler from its harness. He concentrates on braking smoothly, and manages in this way to safeguard her sleep until they bump once, twice, over the sleeping policemen in the street outside her house. She blinks like an old tortoise, sits up straight, clasps her handbag with both hands, runs her tongue round her front teeth, pretends she has never not been awake.

'Do the sleeping policemen work?' he asks, as she fumbles her front-door key in the lock.

'Do they heck as like. You'd think it was the dodgems round here.'

Inside, it's a matter of moments only to light the gas fire and put the kettle on. She comes back, unwrapping her scarf, to find him sitting in one of the armchairs staring at the regular blue buds of flame. 'I thought we'd just have a sandwich,' she says. 'If that's all right?'

'Fine.'

While she's making them, he looks round the room at the photographs. Nick's mother and Auntie Frieda as children, himself in his graduation gown, Miranda at various stages of development from newborn baby onwards. The photographs of Miranda stop abruptly at the time of the divorce. He must bring her some more up-to-date ones, he thinks, but then he's hurt because several of the early photographs are of Barbara and Miranda together, but there are none of Fran and Jasper. When he first asked if he could bring Fran to see her, Frieda had said, 'Leave it a bit, Nick. You know I'm mebbe a bit old-fashioned.' It had spread to include even Jasper. She always asks after him, but it's never 'How's my bairn?' as it used to be with Miranda.

'Is there anything you need doing while I'm here?' he says, hovering in the kitchen door while she slaps butter on to bread.

'You could change the bulb on the landing if you wouldn't mind.'

Of course he doesn't mind. He's relieved to be doing something that only he can do. He gets the stepladder, says, as Grandad always said at such moments, in his younger days, 'Let there be light,' and there was light. He puts the stepladder back in the bedroom and goes down to eat.

When she comes in with the sandwiches on a tray they talk about Geordie and his illness, Frieda reproaching herself for not having spotted the signs sooner. She seems to think if only she'd got him to the doctor more quickly he might have lived for ever. Once or twice Nick notices slips of the tongue: she talks about 'your dad' when she means *her* dad. Tiredness – she must be absolutely knackered. 'Grandad,' he corrects, gently, but then thinks, Why bother? She's only unconsciously recognizing a truth.

When his father died, Nick stood by the grave, eyes stinging, not from grief, but from a kind of despair at his failure to feel anything. His deepest reaction had been one of relief: that he wouldn't have to try to talk to him any more. Cars and cricket, cricket and cars. They'd sit on either side of the fire during Nick's disgracefully rare visits, like a couple of bookends with no book worth reading in the middle.

Once the sandwiches have been eaten and the tray taken away, he asks, 'How bad are the nights?'

He sees her hesitate, the struggle between loyalty and desperation painful to witness. 'Bad,' she says at last.

'Nightmares?'

'Worse than that. He wakes up and it's still happening. I can remember him being like this when I was a little girl. I used to stand at the kitchen door and watch your gran try and get him back into the house. But he'd got over it, that's what I can't understand. He hasn't had turns like that for years. And now it seems like it's all coming back. You know, he thinks he sees Harry being killed. But the thing is, it's not like he's remembering it, it's like he's actually seeing it. He's shouting "Harry" and waving his arms about and when you get hold of him he doesn't see you, he's in a world of his own. To be honest I've been frightened of him once or twice and it's an awful thing because he never once lifted a finger to any of us when I was little. He was never a violent man.'

'Look, when he comes out, I'll do the nights.'

'You can't,' she says immediately. 'When's the baby due?'

'Not till October. I can manage the first few weeks.' To himself he's thinking (hoping?) that a few weeks may be all that's needed. Shepherd said he could go any time. 'You need your rest,' he says. 'You can't do nights and days.'

She blinks doubtfully. 'Well, if you're sure. I can't say it wouldn't be a help, 'cos it would.'

On his way back to the hospital, Nick calls at Geordie's house to check that everything's all right. It's typical of Geordie that he won't surrender his independence and go to live with his daughter, though there's never a week goes past that Frieda doesn't try to persuade him. 'No,' he says. 'I'm all right as I am.'

And until recently he was. He lives in a terrace of two-up, two-down houses, in what used to be a poor district, though now it's rising rapidly as young professional people move in. It's an attractive area, only a short drive from the city centre, yet the houses back on to woods and fields.

The house smells cold, musty and unlived in, though Geordie's only been in hospital a week. Nick checks the windows and the back door, but everything's secure. He goes upstairs, switches on the light in Grandad's bedroom, not knowing what he's doing here. Wanting some contact perhaps, some feeling of closeness that he doesn't get from that semi-stranger in the hospital bed.

Two books on the bedside table. One's called *Soldier, from the Wars Returning* and includes an interview with Geordie, though that's not why it's there. It's there because of the inscription on the title page, *To Geordie, with love and admiration, Helen.*

The other's a scrapbook for cuttings of his public appearances. Not many recent cuttings, only one in the last three months, but before that they come thick and fast. Grandad at the Imperial War Museum, talking to children in schools and colleges, on a televised trip to the battlefields, framed by the arches of Thiepval. The record of an ordinary man who, by living long, had become extraordinary.

On the table beside the wardrobe there's a photograph of two young men in uniform, not obviously brothers, though they were brothers. Tinted sepia, drained of life and colour, as if the mud's already reaching out to claim them. Born to die, that's the impression, though only one of them did. Harry's the one who copped it, dead in 1916, just before the Somme. Yet in the photograph the shadow of what's to come seems to lie over them both. Eighteen years old, a self-conscious moustache framing his upper lip, Grandad looks closer to death than he did this afternoon, 101 years old, riddled with cancer, lying in a hospital bed.

Beside it there's another photograph, a glossy Polaroid taken by Nick on a visit they'd made, earlier this year, to the battlefields. The last week of February, snow on the ground. No time for a man of Geordie's age to be travelling, but they both knew this would be his last time, and that if they didn't seize the chance to go together then, they would never go at all.

Grandad's last, Nick's first, visit. He'd resisted this for years, but now couldn't refuse. At intervals, as once when Grandad stood on the lip of a crater, looking down, it strikes Nick with the force of revelation, though he's known it all his life: *he was there.*

Nothing Nick had heard, nothing he had read, prepared him for the cemeteries. He wandered round, taking surreptitious photographs of Geordie, neither of them speaking much, content to leave each other alone. They visited the cemeteries promiscuously, in no particular order. One of Nick's clearest memories is of Geordie standing in a German cemetery, the thin dark crosses casting blue shadows on the snow, like the footprints of birds.

Just as nothing had prepared him for the cemeteries, so the cemeteries, with their neatly tended plots and individual inscriptions, failed to prepare him for the annihilating abstractions of Thiepval. Geordie walked in a straight line towards the monument, dwarfed by its immensity, his figure shadowy in the faint mist that lingered on the grass. Nick retreated to a curved stone bench, ignoring the damp seeping through the seat of his jeans, and stared at the inscription: TO THE MISSING OF THE SOMME.

He was repelled by it. The monument towered over the landscape, but it didn't soar as a cathedral does. The arches found the sky empty and returned to earth; they opened on to emptiness. It reminded Nick, appropriately enough, of a warrior's helmet with no head inside. No, worse than that: Golgotha, the place of a skull. If, as Nick believed, you should go to the past, looking not for messages or warnings, but simply to be humbled by the weight of human experience that has preceded the brief flicker of your own few days, then Thiepval succeeded brilliantly.

Following in Geordie's footsteps, he walked across the grass and up the steps to the stone of sacrifice, feeling the weight of that experience heavy on the back of his neck. Above him, on the vast flat surfaces the complex structure was designed to provide, were columns of names, stretching up precisely as far as the eye could see. Through the arch was yet another cemetery. 'Inconnu' on the French crosses, 'Known Unto God' on the British stones. Out there were the graves of men whose bodies had become separated from their names; inside the monument thousands of names that had become separated from anything at all. A scrap of blue or khaki cloth. A splinter of charred bone. Nothing else remained. Echoing footsteps, lists of names, arches opening on to emptiness. It seemed to Nick that this place represented not a triumph *over* death, but the triumph *of* death.

Geordie stood for a full ten minutes looking up at Harry's name, and his lips moved, causing Nick to wonder what could be left to say after so many years. Then he went to lay his wreath on the steps of the altar, standing bare-headed, while outside it began to snow again, small stinging flakes whirling about on a bitter wind. Nick stood beside him. Up to that moment he'd always disliked the easy sentiment of poppy symbolism, but then he became grateful for it, for into that abstract space, with its columns of names and its ungraspable figures, the poppies brought the colour of blood.

Geordie was attempting to graft his memories on to Nick – that's what the visit was about – and perhaps, in spite of Nick's resistance, he'd come close to succeeding. Something important happened to Nick at Thiepval and he'd never come to terms with it. There'd never been time. As soon as they got back Geordie started to feel ill, as if the accomplishment of that final visit had given his body permission to let go. At first tiredness, then changes in bowel function, then a constant sensation of heaviness. Nick knew before the results of the tests came through, and he suspected Geordie knew as well. But all Geordie ever said was: 'It's the bayonet wound playing me up.'

If Nick hadn't gone to France he might have regarded

Geordie's theory as merely ignorant, but he'd stood beside him in the empty arches of Thiepval, looking up at Harry's name on the wall, and from that perspective Geordie's belief in the power of old wounds to leak into the present was not so easily dismissed.

In the hospital Nick stares blankly at the empty bed. He isn't prepared for this. How can they not have been told? Why didn't they ring? But perhaps they did. Perhaps they rang Frieda, but she couldn't contact him. A nurse squeaks up on rubber-soled shoes. 'Are you looking for Mr Lucas?'

'Yes.'

'He's in a side ward.'

Nick goes back along the ward, where men anonymous in pyjamas turn to stare at him as he walks past. He stares through the portholes in the doors of the side wards, and spots him at last. He pushes the door open. The sides of the bed have been raised. It looks as if he's lying in a cot. Eyes tightly closed, humiliation visible in every muscle of his clenched jaw.

'How are you, Grandad?' Nick smells the sourness of sweat on his skin as he bends to give him a hug.

A nurse follows him into the room. 'He was in the sluice room last night at two o'clock,' she says. 'Weren't you, love?'

Geordie doesn't answer her.

'What were you doing in there?' Nick asks after she's withdrawn and left them alone.

'God knows.'

'Dreaming?'

'Something like that.'

Nick thinks: I can't bear this, and a second later is appalled by the selfishness of his response. If Grandad can bear it, he can.

'It's the pills,' Geordie says. 'I've never been one for pills.'

It's not the pills, and they both know it, but somehow the hospital prescribes the kind of conversation they can have with each other. Nick just wants to see Geordie back in his own home, in his own bed, as fast as possible. 'I forgot to mention it this afternoon,' he says. 'Helen wants to know when she can come and see you?' When there's no reply he adds, 'You remember Helen?'

'Of course I remember Helen, I'm not daft.'

'What shall I tell her?'

'I don't want her seeing me like this.'

He always made a fuss when Helen was coming. Got bathed, shaved, wore a suit and a tie. Frieda used to say, 'Look at him, all done up like a shilling dinner. His girlfriend must be coming,' and bizarrely, behind the teasing, there was real jealousy.

'Give it a few days,' he says now, reluctantly, and then, abruptly, brings up the real problem. 'I want these bloody bars down. I'm like a ruddy great baby sat up in a cot. I can't have anybody seeing me like this.'

'They'll put them down in the morning.'

'They'd better. If they don't I'm out of here.'

Nick grips his wrist through the bars. 'I should be going now. I'll see you at the weekend.'

'Aye. Perhaps.'

'Now what's that supposed to mean?'

No answer.

'Auntie Frieda'll be in tomorrow.'

Nick hovers, knowing that in his grandfather's position he would find this lingering impossibly irritating. He bends down and holds the thin shoulders whose bones seem to become a little more prominent every day. Old soldiers never die – they only fade away. Though the man who shouts and rages and cries out for Harry in the kitchen or the sluice room isn't fading away, whatever else he's doing. 'I'll ring and see how you're getting on,' he says inadequately, and then walks out down the grey shining corridor, past the WRVS stall with its flowers and balloons and fruit, and out into the car-park, where the stars burn pale against the sodium orange of the lights.

SEVEN

At the exit from the motorway Nick hesitates, then, to the immense irritation of the driver behind him, flicks his indicator from right to left and drives to a row of terraced houses not far from the University library. Four-storey substantial Victorian houses, divided into elegant, expensive flats. Helen has the top floor of one of them. A beech tree, its leaves a virulent green in the light from the street lamp, reaches to her windows.

Nick knocks, hears the television news switched off and then Helen appears, barefoot, in jeans and T-shirt, short dark hair spiked around her ears. 'Nick,' she says. 'How are you?'

'Not so bad.'

'Come in.'

This is what he needs, he realizes, following her through into the living room, though it's probably not what he ought to need.

'Coffee?'

'Please.'

'Or beer?'

'Beer would be better.'

The fridge door bangs shut. She comes back into the room hugging cans with a cold sweat on them to her chest, and hands one over. 'Here you are.'

Sweeping piles of books off the sofa on to the floor, she peels open her own can and applies her mouth to the white foam that bubbles out, laughing and flicking beer from her hands as she sits back. 'So how are you really?'

'All right.'

She waits. Don't pull that one, he thinks. I do the silences.

'Geordie's dying.'

'Oh, Nick, I am sorry.'

'You're the only one.' This comes out so much more bitter than he intended that he reins himself back. 'Well, you know, I get a bit fed up with people saying, Perhaps it's for the best, he's had a good innings . . .'

'You'll miss him.'

'Yes.'

'So will I.' She attempts a smile. 'Won't have anybody to flirt with now.'

'Oh, you'll find somebody, I expect.'

'What's wrong?'

'Cancer. They've done an exploratory operation. Secondaries all over the place.'

'Is he having radiotherapy?'

'There's no point. It'd just mess him about, and it wouldn't give him that much longer anyway.'

'Can I see him?'

'Give it a few days,' Nick says awkwardly. 'The thing is they've put the sides of the bed up and he's so upset about that he can't think about anything else.' He hesitates, because telling anybody this, even Helen, seems like a betrayal. 'He's taken to wandering about in the middle of the night.'

'But he's not confused. Not when I saw him.'

'No, but you can see why they think he is. He's back there. Poor old Frieda gets mistaken for the German army. I mean, I don't think it's confusion because I think he'd be showing signs of it the rest of the time. It sounds like flashbacks, but why should he suddenly start doing that again?'

'Fear of death? Pretty powerful trigger.'

'I don't know.'

'How's he going to manage?'

'Frieda'll look after him during the day – he's all right then – I'll do the nights.'

'And what does Fran think about that?'

'She doesn't know yet.'

'Sure you wouldn't rather have a whisky?'

He smiled. 'I think I'll take you up on that. But only a small one, I'm driving.'

'You could walk from here.'

'If I turned up sozzled I would be in trouble.'

'Small one, I promise.'

While she's out of the room, Nick passes the time looking along her bookshelves and, for the second time that evening, identifies the red cover of *Soldier, from the Wars Returning*. This time he opens it and Geordie's voice leaps off the page.

GEORDIE: Like Rip Van bloody Winkle, I suppose. You don't hear that story much now, do you? We got told it at school. Friday afternoons, we used to have a story, last lesson before the bell, and that one sort of stuck in me mind. I remember walking home from school – four miles, it was, there and back twice a day – they'd think it was child abuse these days – and thinking all the time about this man going to sleep on the hillside, and waking up years later, and nobody knowing who he was. It haunted me. I used to think it was awful.

HELEN: What in particular?

GEORDIE: The loneliness.

Helen's focus in the book was on the interaction between the individual veteran's memories of his combat experience, and the changing public perception of the war. Geordie, from the moment she met him, intrigued her, not merely because he was old enough to remember the trenches, and remembered them clearly, but because he had, at different stages of his life, coped with his memories in radically different ways.

As a young man just back from France, Geordie refused to talk about the war, and avoided all reminders of it. Every November he wore a poppy, but he took no part in Armistice Day commemorations. Instead he went for a long walk in the country, returning well after dark, exhausted and silent as ever. Refused all questions. When obliged to speak stammered so badly he could barely make himself understood. This was the man Nick remembered.

Then, in the sixties, Geordie began to talk about the war. Over the next three decades his willingness to share his memories increased and, as other veterans died around him, his own rarity value grew. In the nineties he was one of a tiny group of survivors who gathered for the anniversaries of the first day of the Somme, and most of the others were in wheelchairs. There were rewards in this for him. He was sought after, listened to, he had friends, interests, a purpose in life at an age when old people are too often sitting alone in chilly rooms waiting for their relatives to phone. But the sense of mission was genuine. His message was simple: *It happened once, therefore it can happen again. Take care.*

And the stammer? The stammer vanished or, at least, was reduced to a slight hesitation that had the effect of concentrating his listeners' attention on the next word.

Helen was interested in the reasons for these changes, in the social forces that had obliged the young Geordie to repress his memories of fear, pain, bitterness, degradation, because what he had thought and felt at that time was not acceptable. A later generation, fresh from a visit to *Oh! What a Lovely War*, the *Dies Irae* of Britten's *War Requiem* pounding in its ears, couldn't get enough of fear, pain, etc. The horror, the horror. Give us more. Suddenly a large part of Geordie's experience was 'acceptable', though still not all.

Towards the end of the published interview, Helen attempted to get Geordie to see that he still hadn't been asked to talk about class, the different experiences of officers and men, profiteering, the whole idea of the war as a business in which some people suffered and died to make others rich, though this bitterness, as much as the anguish of grief for lost comrades, had shaped and framed his experience of the post-war years. He was still, Helen believed, remaking his memories to fit in with public perceptions of the war, only now he was working to a different template.

She tried to get Geordie to frame his war experience in terms of late-twentieth-century preoccupations. Gender. Definitions of masculinity. Homoeroticism. Homo-*what*? asked Geordie. Helen, with her Oxford First. Geordie, with his board-school education, shovelled into one dead-end job at the age of fourteen and then, aged eighteen, into another. It was an unequal contest. Geordie won.

'Penny for them?' Helen says.

Nick feels cold glass against his fingers and takes the

whisky. 'Oh, I was just thinking about this.' He shows her the book. 'I don't suppose you've still got the transcripts, have you?'

'Yes, somewhere. In the department, I think.'

'May I borrow them? I mean, I'd get them photocopied and let you have them back.'

'No problem. I'll look them out.' She curls up on the sofa, and chinks the ice in her glass. 'You know, I went with him to the Imperial War Museum and he was in the trench talking to these kids and they were saying, "Was it like this?" And he was saying, "Well, this is pretty good, but in the real trenches there were rats and dead bodies and horrible smells, and bombs falling and it was cold and it was wet and it was noisy and you were fed up and you were frightened and you wanted to go home." And of course the kids lapped it up. There were two little boys racing up and down the trench making machine-gun noises. You know?' She rakes the room with an imaginary machine-gun. 'And I said to Geordie, "Are you sure this is doing any good?"'

'And he said?'

'"Yes."' She laughs. 'He never doubted it.'

Silence. Nick takes a gulp of whisky and waits for the question he knows is coming.

'What do you think?'

'I'm not a historian.'

'No, but you must have an opinion.'

'Well, you see the first thing is I don't believe in

public memory. A memory's a biochemical change in an individual brain, and that's all there is. There's quite a lot of evidence that traumatic memories are stored in a different part of the brain from normal memories, and that's what makes them so incredibly persistent. And so . . . almost hallucinatory. They're not accessible to language in the same way. It's like watching a film, or . . . or even worse it's like acting in a film.' He spreads his hands. 'As for warnings and messages . . . I don't know.' A spurt of anger. 'Anyway what *is* the message? You look back over the whole horrible blood-sodden mess. Isn't the real message: *You can get away with it.*?'

"And yet you went to the battlefields with him.'

'Somebody had to. He couldn't have managed on his own.' Nick wants to tell her about Thiepval, but there's no time, he ought to be going. And anyway he hasn't succeeded in telling himself about Thiepval yet. 'Thanks.' He puts down the empty glass. 'I needed that.'

'I'll look out the transcripts,' she says, opening the door. 'And you'll let me know when he's ready for a visit?'

The August night's cool, rather than cold, yet he shivers, an automatic reaction to the glitter of moonlight on cobbles and the stars pricking sharply through the telegraph wires that score the sky. The car smells musty, a mess of cardboard cartons left from the family's last outing litters the back seats. Curried chips, his nose tells him. Gareth's favourite. He wonders as he fumbles with the ignition key if he's fit to drive. He's well under the limit for alcohol, but he seems to be getting more tired by the minute, as if all the energy he'd expended over the last few weeks, moving and decorating, had been borrowed and the loan's just been called in. His hands hurt where the wallpaper scraper rubbed off the skin. He yawns and yawns again, as the car at last sputters into life. He'll go the back way, he decides. It's a bit longer, but, at this time of night, there'll be next to no traffic.

It's been raining. There are crescents of silver light trapped inside the drops that speckle the glass. It seems a pity to press the button and sweep them away. Almost as soon as he starts the engine the rain comes on heavier. Smears of orange light on greasy cobbles, the wipers' swish and whine, make it hard to stay alert. He's hunched over the wheel peering at the edges of the road for guidance, driving as if in a thick fog, though there's no more than a slight mist.

What he wanted to say to Helen, but couldn't find a tactful way of phrasing it, was that she'd got Geordie all wrong. That she was so much in love with her thesis that she distorted his experience to make it fit. Geordie's memories aren't malleable: they don't change to fit other people's perceptions of the war. On the contrary. Geordie's tragedy is that his memories are carved in granite. The nightmares of Harry's death that had Geordie screaming back in 1919 are the same ones that wake him, sweating and terrified, in the sluice room now. And secretly, what he wants to say is that raking about in the detritus of other people's memories is a waste of time and energy. The only true or useful thing that can be said about the past is that it's over. It no longer exists.

All the houses are in darkness. Lob's Hill, when he gets back, will be in darkness. Fran will have given up and gone to bed by now, and she won't be too pleased either. He'd said he was going out 'for a few hours'. His headlights pick out the silver trunks of trees, moths flickering like beads of light, big, pale stars of bindweed, and then, in the rear mirror, darkness swallows them. His lights seem to create the road he drives along, and then consign it to oblivion.

He lets himself gain speed, sits back, starts to relax. Too much, he's getting drowsy. Probably he should pull over and walk up and down a bit, but that would make him even later than he is and anyway he's nearly home. Another few minutes and then, providing Jasper's asleep, he can slide into bed and lose consciousness. Louder music, that's the thing.

He's tapping on the wheel when a girl emerges from a gap between the trees and runs out into the road. A pale face turned towards him, staring through the windscreen. Not terrified, not anything, blank. The features shadowless, whited out by the glare. There's a second when Nick knows it's too late, knows it coldly and clearly and, despite the bulging of his heart, calmly. Nothing he can do, neither braking nor swerving, will be in time. The girl slips silently under his wheels.

A few yards further on the car skids to a halt. Automatically he puts the handbrake on and reaches for the door, dreading screams or, worse, silence. Already he's out of the car and running, searching for the hump, the dark shape, in the road, his eyes blinded by the headlights. He can make nothing of the confused mêlée of moonlight and shadows. Except that the road's empty. Thrown into the hedge? He searches on either side, groping through grass and stinging nettles. His grass-snarled feet send up a cloud of small pale moths, but his eyes, his hands, find nothing. He runs back to the car, gropes underneath. Warm tar under his fingertips, greasy from the recent shower, still squishy from the long hours of sun. He prods round the wheels. Nothing. Crawls out again, runs his hands along the bumper. The headlights are burning his retinas, he can't see a bloody thing, relies on his fingers to tell him the cool curve of metal is intact.

It's impossible. He'd hit a dog once, a young Labrador, and the whole bonnet had crumpled under the impact. There's no way the car can be undamaged. The headlights throw his distorted shadow far up the road. Unless there was no impact. He thinks back, and he's almost sure he neither heard nor felt an impact. Nor had he felt the bump of the wheels going over a body. He bends down, shaking, finds sweetheart sticking to the legs of his trousers and peels it off, automatically, trying to think. No impact, and since he'd seen the girl fall under the wheels, no impact meant no girl. Hypnogogic hallucination. Must have been, can't have been anything else. He'd been drowsy, mesmerized by the swish of wipers and the flick-flickering of his lights across the trees.

What should he do? He sits in the driver's seat with his feet on the road and lights a cigarette. Go to the police? He'll be breathalized. Well, he's all right, he's pretty sure he's all right. In any case that's not the point. The point is there's been no accident. There's nothing to report. He double checks the bumper. Nothing could hit the car without leaving some trace, and the bumper's unscathed. He lets the relief wash over him, ashamed, a second later, that he could have run round like that, gasping and panicking, not thinking at all.

He tries to recall the girl, but her face was whited out by the glare of the headlights. An impression of long hair and a long skirt, as she came running out from the trees. Nothing more individual than that. Where had she been running to? The only house on this stretch of road is Lob's Hill. Though if she's the product of an over-tired mind, it makes no sense to ask where she was running to.

The house is in darkness when he arrives. He goes to the living room first, spends a few moments looking at the painting, and then slowly, unbuttoning his shirt, climbs the stairs. His mind fizzes. He can smell his armpits, a fear-sweat smell unlike any other, and despises himself for it. On the landing he undresses and then, naked, goes into the bedroom.

EIGHT

Fran sees a silhouette against the landing light, sharply black and slim, so that for a moment, waking from deep sleep, she feels a jolt of fear. Almost unconsciously she moves to give him room as he climbs into bed, and begins groping for sleep again, only to realize he's lying awake beside her, flat on his back, his skin, where his thigh touches hers, burning hot. Grandfather ill, cancer, she remembers. 'How is he?'

'Bad.'

She mumbles some kind of response.

'I had a bit of a shock on the way back. I thought I'd hit something.'

'But you didn't?'

'No, it's all right.'

Rabbits and hedgehogs and the occasional bird lie in crumpled and bloody heaps all along the back lane that leads from their house to the main road. It's awful, but what can you do? She squeezes his hand in token consolation and turns away. He curls around her, and after a few seconds she feels the stir and rise of his cock.

'Nick.'

'I know, I know.' He presses his face into the hollow between her shoulder blades, lifting her hair and running his mouth from side to side, a slow sweeping kiss. A hand comes round, cradling her breasts, fingertips find her nipples, tweak gently.

'I wouldn't do that, if I were you,' Fran says dryly. 'You might get more than you bargain for.'

They lie tensely locked together; she waits for him to give up and turn away, but he doesn't, and part of her's thinking, It's not much fun for him. He does try to help, only now he's got his grandfather to worry about, and he just seems to look on helplessly as control of the domestic situation slithers out of her grasp. Between them, Jasper and the unborn baby are eating her alive.

Responding to her tension, the baby heaves itself across her stomach, one of its cosmonaut somersaults. It's nobody's fault, she thinks, and it won't go on for ever, but meanwhile Nick hasn't had sex for weeks, months, and almost involuntarily she arches her back, giving him an easier entrance. 'I won't move,' Nick says. 'I'll just lodge him inside.' And she wants to giggle at his self-deception, does giggle, and he gasps as he feels the nudge of her downward-shaken womb. He begins to move, tentatively, asking on held breath, 'You all right?' 'Fine,' she says, still sleepily, then starts to get interested. She likes this position, though generally, after a few minutes, they switch to her lying over the edge of the bed and Nick kissing her, but his thrusts become faster and deeper, his hand on her hip braces and tightens, and then with a cry he's shuddering and jerking and pouring himself into her. Painful tweaking of the skin on her hips follows as he cries out and convulses and sobs, yes *sobs*, and what the fuck, she thinks, do you have to sob about?

Afterwards they lie side by side on their backs, staring into the dark. He says, 'That was all right, wasn't it?' and she says, 'Was it?'

'I didn't know whether you wanted to come.'

'You didn't try to find out.'

'I could kiss you down there. Come on, Fran, please . . . Please?'

'Don't bother.'

She turns over. After lying for a while, irritatingly exuding guilt, Nick rolls away from her, and though she tosses and turns and heaves deep sighs it's not long before he starts to snore.

When she wakes next morning he's still snoring.

He'll be full of guilt when he wakes up.

Not full enough.

Today's Sunday and they're going for a day out to Fleete House, where, Nick seems to think, the Fanshawes lived after they left Lob's Hill. But the thought of having to organize it all: the nappies, the sandwiches, the orange juice, the cans of coke, the car seat, the pushchair, the beaker, the potty – in case Jasper starts to think its absence means he needn't bother – makes her want to vomit.

Lying there, lazily, in the last few minutes before Jasper wakes and roars for attention, she dips her fingers between her legs and sniffs them. That warm, kippery smell of fucked-the-night-before cunt, the best smell in the world. Normally she'd have invited Nick to join in, but not after last night. Her fingers move further down to the episiotomy scar, soon to be cut open for the third time. She wonders how Nick would react if somebody proposed cutting his scrotum open without a general anaesthetic and then repeating the procedure, twice. He isn't keen on the idea of a vasectomy – the Big Snip, he calls it – though it's the obvious solution for somebody who grows ten thumbs at the sight of a Durex packet.

Jasper's chuntering rises to a yell. Fran gets out of bed, staggers out into the landing, feeling dizzy as she always does when she gets up too quickly, and trips over the tangle of jeans and underpants Nick's left on the landing. He'd only got undressed out there because he was trying not to disturb her, but that doesn't stop her feeling angry. Lifting the heap of clothes on one bare foot, she kicks it halfway downstairs.

Jasper's leaning on the rail of his cot in that four-square John Bull way, the way a man stands when he's inordinately proud of what he's got between his legs, though what Jasper's got is a sodden nappy that drops to the floor with a disgusting plop as she picks him up. 'You stink,' she says. His bottom's wet and cold against her arm, as she carries him along the corridor to the bathroom – pausing to bang on Gareth's door as she goes past – and runs the bath.

The bathroom's lovely, almost her favourite room in the house, though the window's so closed around with roses that the room seems dark. Green, rather. A submarine light with fugitive shadows of leaves chasing each other across the wall.

She runs a shallow bath and puts Jasper in. It's easier to hose him down than to wipe him. 'You're going to see Paddington Bear today,' she tells him. He's concentrating on a yellow plastic duck that, when squeezed, squirts jets of water high into the air. One spurt hits her in the eye, and he roars with laughter as she gasps and blinks. Like father, like son, she thinks, and lifts him out to dry.

Gareth ignores the bang on the door. With any luck he'll get half an hour on the new game, before Mum bursts in rabbiting on about family togetherness and all that crap. The screen glows gently in the gloom of the closed curtains. While he waits for the computer to finish loading, he reads the back of the box.

There is no doubt that you are being watched, by whom and by what life form is not determined. Even Spock has not been able to accurately assess this data. The occurrences are just too strange. Is that truly an ancient WWI triplane heading straight for you at Warp 9? How can your sensors suddenly report life forms on a dead planet . . . ?

He feels pressure on the back of his neck. The sense of somebody in the room behind him's so strong he almost turns round, thinking it must be Mum telling him to for God's sake switch the damn thing off and get dressed. But she'd have spoken by now, and Gareth's too frightened to turn round.

Instead, he goes on looking straight ahead. He sees his own shadowy reflection in the screen, but can't be sure there's nobody else there. In a small voice he hardly recognizes as his, he says, 'Please go away.'

Nobody answers. After a few moments the pressure on the back of his neck's lifted and he knows he's alone.

'Why do babies need so much stuff?' Nick asks, pushing rolled-up nappies into the plastic duffel bag with its design of blue frolicking teddy bears, while Fran tries to squeeze the potty into the zipped compartment underneath. He knows the answer, he's just trying to break the thunderous silence Fran's maintained since breakfast, but she's in no mood to respond to overtures.

'If you don't mind him shitting on the car seat say so and I'll leave some of it behind.'

'Miran –'

'Yes?'

'Nothing.'

Oh, Fran thinks, I see. Either Barbara managed things better or Miranda was the first baby to be born with a miraculous self-wiping arse. 'Pass the nappy liners, will you?'

Nick hands them over in silence, then goes into the hall to hurry Miranda and Gareth along. Miranda appears at the top of the stairs wearing the same long skirt and T-shirt she's been wearing since she arrived. He wishes she'd make more effort, but he doesn't know how to say so; anyway, she has enough to cope with. There's no sign of Gareth.

'What's Gareth doing?'

'Cleaning his teeth.'

Oh, God. 'Bang on the bathroom door, will you? Tell him we'll go without him.'

Nick goes back into the living room to find Fran struggling with the toggles on another plastic bag. 'Is that it?'

'That's it.'

'Dink,' says Jasper.

'You can't have one,' says Nick.

'Oh, give him one. He'll only scream.'

Nick unpacks the bag, pours orange juice into a beaker and watches as Jasper raises it unsteadily to his lips. He manages without spilling any. 'Good boy,' Nick says, stroking his hair. 'Do you know the fontanel's completely closed now?'

'Are you sure?'

'I think so.'

He investigates Jasper's scalp, pressing gently here and there. Fran comes to look too, and they stare in joint fascination at the small blond head they've produced between them.

'Mum . . . ' Gareth says.

They look up guiltily, as if they've been caught in an illicit threesome, to find the two older children staring at them accusingly from the door.

'OK,' Fran says. 'Get in the car.'

Nick looks at her, at the stained T-shirt and straggly hair, and says, 'You're not going like that?'

Abruptly, she starts to cry. 'It's all very well for you. By the time I've got everything ready there's no time for me.'

The children gawp at her.

'Get in the car!' Nick shouts.

Miranda darts him a reproachful look, then stalks out without a word. Gareth bangs the door.

They're left alone. Nick sits in one of the armchairs and listens to Fran cry, which she does very thoroughly, giving herself up to the sobs. Jasper stares at her, tries an experimental whimper, then moves closer to his father, resting one pudgy fist on his knee.

'What's wrong, Fran? What is it?' Nick asks as a gap in the sobs seems to be approaching.

'I don't know.' She wipes the tears away angrily. 'It's nothing, I'm just tired.'

'Would you like to stay here and get some sleep? I'll cope with them.'

'No, it's all right.' She looks down at herself, at the outstretched, abandoned, puppet legs. 'I just don't like what I've turned into, that's all.'

'It's not for ever.'

She wipes her nose on the back of her hand. 'Feels like it.'

'Be better when we've got the house straight.'

She looks at the wall painting. 'They'd have had servants, wouldn't they? The Fanshawes.'

'I suppose so. No birth control, though, or nothing reliable anyway.'

Ours wasn't, Fran thinks.

'Not that ours was,' Nick says, with an apologetic laugh. 'Still, the Great Snip will be.'

Great snip, she thinks scornfully. You don't know you're born. But she feels friendlier towards him than she has all morning, and by the time she's combed her hair and changed her T-shirt she's able to look out of the window at the milky blue of the sky and think, with some anticipation of pleasure, It's going to be a real scorcher.

'Christ, it's fucking hot,' says Paddington Bear. He's standing on a patch of grass outside a circus tent, and the remark's addressed to nobody in particular.

'Look, Jasper,' Nick says. 'Paddington's waving. Are you going to wave back?'

He half expects Jasper to be frightened of a six-foot-tall

bear in a sou'wester, duffel coat and red wellies, but Jasper takes one look, pulls his hand free of Nick's, and hurls himself on to the wellies with all the abandonment of a rubber fetishist. Paddington bends down, rather clumsily because of the wadding round his middle, and pats Jasper on the head before straightening up and saying, 'Hello, Prof. How you doing?'

'Fine,' Nick replies, trying to place the voice.

'Buddle,' says Paddington in muffled tones. Losing patience, he takes off his head. 'Buddle,' he says again, running his fingers through his sweaty hair.

'Hello,' Nick says.

'Can't get a job,' says Buddle, answering the unspoken question.

'But you got a First.'

'I think that's part of the trouble.'

Buddle notices a family with three children approaching and starts to replace his head. At that moment Jasper looks up, sees a headless bear and screams. Nick picks him up and tries to console him as Buddle lumbers off, shouting loudly, 'Marmalade sandwiches!', 'Luggage labels!' and 'Peru!'

That's what a First in psychology does for you, Nick thinks, hoisting Jasper on to his shoulders and setting off in search of Fran. The position does his neck no good at all, but Jasper loves it, twining his fingers painfully round chunks of hair. Wonder he's not bald. 'Ow, Jasper.' Jasper laughs.

Gareth's walking on stilts, Miranda's juggling with leather balls, kids all round them are skipping and playing skittles. Fran's sitting on the grass watching them, looking a bit better, Nick thinks. 'Come on, let's go to the house. They'll be all right here.'

A steep slope leads to the house. 'Do you think it's the same Fanshawes?' Fran asks.

'I don't see why not.'

'He must have gone up in the world.' She nods to the house that towers over them, against a landscape of wooded hills.

'Yes, well, he did. Made his money in the First World War, munitions. 1919 –' Nick spreads his arms to indicate the grandeur before them.

The question's settled for them as soon as they enter the house, for there, in the hall, is a portrait of Sir William Fanshawe, older, but unmistakably the man on the wall, same keen gaze, same voracious intelligence. Sadder, perhaps. But then we all get sadder, Nick thinks.

'I feel quite embarrassed for him, don't you?' Fran says.

'No – oh, you mean his dick?' Nick's pulling money out of his back pocket. 'No, green with envy, actually.'

The staircase leads to a long gallery, lined with Victorian paintings of no great merit. Wounded animals, blood on their paws, crying children, glistening tears on rounded cheeks, obsessively lingered over.

'I don't like his taste,' Fran says, pausing in front of a dog that's lying in the snow next to its dead master. 'It's very old-fashioned, isn't it? I mean it's old-fashioned for the twenties. You'd think the war had never happened, it's –'

'1898.'

It's not just the war that's missing either. They've passed several portraits of William Fanshawe, one of his first wife, Henrietta, two of his second wife, Isobel, three of the nephew who inherited the estate. But, as they know from the painting in Lob's Hill, Fanshawe had a daughter and two sons. So far there's not been a trace of any of them.

Where are the children?

Fran stops to look into one of the bedrooms. Huge four-poster bed with heavy curtains in a dull green-gold. Chaise longue, writing desk, cheval glass, windows full of sunlight.

'All that and nursery maids and nannies to look after the kids,' Fran says. 'Marvellous.'

'And the husband slept next door.'

'Even better.'

'Only you'd wake up and he'd be standing at the foot of the bed in his nightshirt demanding his conjugal rights.'

'Oh, yeah? What's changed?'

Ouch. 'Fran, I –'

'It's all right.'

It isn't – the cursory brush of her mouth over his tells him so – but she's trying. They both are.

Three ornate rooms further on and Jasper's thoroughly

fed up, grizzling and stamping his feet. Fran kneels to comfort him and he hits her in the eye.

'Hey!' Nick says, shaking his arm. 'You don't do that.'

'I'd better take him out.'

'Do you mind if I stay a bit?'

'No, go on. I'll be at the tent.'

'I won't be long. Five minutes.'

As soon as he's left alone Nick plunges into the maze of corridors, scanning the walls, peering into bedrooms, at paintings, at clusters of photographs on dressing tables, looking for a clue, any clue, to the secret of the house.

There's nothing on the first floor, nothing in the bedrooms, where intimate family snapshots might be displayed, nothing on the staircase or in the main hall, where large-scale portraits of Fanshawe, his wives and other members of his family line the walls. Then, near the main entrance, opening off to the left, Nick comes across Fanshawe's study. A printed notice by the door says that his desk is exactly as he left it when he went upstairs on the night of his death. Nick leans across the rope that closes off the room from visitors. It's very quiet. A guided tour has just gone past and left the hall empty. Too quickly to feel any surprise at his own action, though normally he's the most law-abiding of men, Nick unhooks the rope and goes into the room.

Tall windows behind the desk open on to a vista of wooded hills. Touching the back of Fanshawe's chair, Nick sees Fanshawe's signature in mirror writing on the blotter. A clock, stamps, stacks of paper, envelopes – no photographs.

But Nick's already lost interest in the desk, for he can see from his new position that the room's L-shaped, though the horizontal bar of the L is so short it's hardly more than an alcove. Nick slips into it, with relief, because now he can't be seen from the door.

He turns. There, hanging on the wall where nobody in the house can see it, is not *a* portrait, but *the* portrait, the photograph on which the wall painting in Lob's Hill was unmistakably based. The boy, who here seems merely sullen and rebellious, rests his hand on his father's shoulder. The girl looks unhappy, perhaps, but Isobel's obviously proud of her small son, and Fanshawe – Fanshawe's simply himself, alert, energetic, avid.

A fine family. That's what anybody, on the evidence of this photograph, would think, so why put it here where almost nobody would ever see it? Even Fanshawe, if he wanted to look at it, would have had to get up from his desk and go into the alcove. He could never glance up from his desk and be surprised by this. Why? Because the sight of his children was, for some reason, painful? Because he needed to brace himself to look at them? Nick's gaze tracks from one young face to the next, and a gust of despair sweeps over him. Not his own – Fanshawe's.

Quickly and cautiously, Nick leaves the room, hooks the rope back across the door, and goes out through the main entrance on to the lawn, lifting his face to the warmth of the sun, as if the chill that lingers on his skin could be so easily dispelled.

The inside of the tent glows yellow with sunlight, and there's a smell of hot grass under canvas, a smell that recalls some childhood excitement, though Nick can't place the memory.

Adults on chairs at the back, kids cross-legged at the front. Two men in orange overalls stagger in carrying mops and buckets. Much hitting of each other's bums with broom handles follows, greeted by gales of laughter from the younger children. The shorter of the two, blubbing loudly, climbs on to the knee of the youngest and prettiest mother and demands to have his bottom kissed better. It's all very well done. Howls of pain to please the kids, just enough innuendo to stop Dad nodding off to sleep. Though this particular Dad's badly in need of a cigarette. He touches Fran's arm and points to the door.

Outside he decides to see if he can buy a guidebook. Fran likes them: if Jasper's playing up she sometimes sees more of a place later in the guidebook than she does when she's there. He goes across to the converted stables and finds the shop almost empty. Everybody's either in the circus tent or sitting outside the restaurant at tables in the sun. Nick asks for the official guide, but finds they've sold out. Disappointed, he makes do with postcards, and then goes across to the books section and searches for something on the Fanshawes.

He's given up and is just about to leave when he sees a book called *Mary Ann Cotton's Teapot and Other Notable Northern Murders*, by Veronica Laidlaw. He knows Veronica slightly, having met her once or twice at college dinners. She's a rather prolific historical novelist, but he had no idea she was interested in crime. This had been published in 1995 by the Vindolanda Press. The cover has a picture of Mary Ann carrying the infamous teapot, which contained, or so she always claimed, right up to the steps of the gallows, nothing but fortifying herbal infusions. Lying on a bed in the background of the picture, about to be fortified, was one or other of her various husbands.

If everybody connected to Mary Ann Cotton who died suddenly from gastrointestinal upsets was actually murdered, she is easily the most deadly of British killers. But of course we don't know that. Many of her children, according to their death certificates, died of 'teething'; and some of these deaths may have been natural. Nick knows about her through Geordie, who remembers his sister Mary and the other little lasses singing a skipping rhyme.

Mary Ann Cotton, she's dead and she's rotten.
She lies in the grave with her eyes wide oppen.
Sing! Sing! Oh what shall I sing?
Mary Ann Cotton is hung up with string.

Where? Where?
Up in the air.
Selling black puddings a penny a pair.

He also remembers being put in a dark cupboard under the stairs when he was naughty and being told that Mary Ann Cotton would get him.

It's worth buying, Nick thinks, for that reason alone. The garish cover's misleading. Veronica's treatment of her selected crimes is anything but sensational.

Mary Ann Cotton is dealt with in the second chapter, the first being devoted to the gibbeting of William Jobling at Jarrow Slake. The last chapter is on Mary Bell, an eleven-year-old girl who, in 1968, killed two small boys, one of them on the Tin Lizzie, a stretch of waste land less than a mile from Lob's Hill. Nick remembers the case: the air of gloom that spread throughout the city, though by contemporary standards media attention had been restrained.

Nick wanders out into the sunshine to read it. He can't think of any other 'notable northern murders', and flicks through the intervening pages until his attention is caught by the name: Fanshawe. With a slight drying of the mouth, he turns to the beginning of the chapter – Chapter Five – and reads: 'The Murder of James Fanshawe at Lob's Hill'.

James Fanshawe was two years old at the time of his death, the only child of the second marriage of William

Fanshawe, a local armaments manufacturer. By his first marriage, William had another son, Robert, aged eleven at the time of the murder, and a daughter Muriel, who was aged thirteen. Neither of the children of the first marriage liked their stepmother, and both seem to have been jealous of their half-brother, James.

On the morning of 5 November 1904 Jessie Baines, the nursery maid, went into the nursery and found James's bed empty. Normally she would have been sleeping in the nursery with him, but she had a bad cough, and his sister Muriel had slept in his room instead. James was a nervous child, frightened of the dark, and still more frightened of the shadows cast by his night-light. His first word, pointing at the shadows, had been 'sadda'. Jessie shook Muriel awake, but she was difficult to rouse and seemed unaware of her surroundings. James was nowhere to be found and the police were called to the house.

At almost the same time as James's bed was found empty, a boy from Tidmarsh Street, playing truant from school in order to guard the street bonfire from rival gangs who might steal from it or set it alight, crawled inside the open space at the heart of the fire, and found himself confronted by the body of a fair-haired toddler. The Guy's mask had been placed over his face, perhaps to hide the terrible injuries underneath, but blood had seeped through.

The Fanshawes were immediately informed of the

discovery, and shortly afterwards William Fanshawe identified the dead boy as James. There were no signs of a forced entry to the house, though the front door, which William Fanshawe distinctly remembered locking, was open.

William and Isobel Fanshawe slept together. The two maids shared a bedroom in the attic. That left Robert, sleeping by himself, and Muriel, sleeping in James's room. She had taken cough medicine, she said, thinking that her cough was keeping James awake. She had seen and heard nothing. Robert's story was even simpler. He had gone to bed and gone to sleep. The next thing he knew Jessie was screaming. He had, however, noticed a tramp hanging about in the lane behind the house several days previously, though he had not thought to mention it to anybody at the time. Muriel had seen him too, or so she said. They described a scruffy villainous-looking man with a scar down one cheek, the sort of figure who could not possibly have passed unnoticed. Nobody else had seen him.

The Fanshawes were well known, and news of the murder spread quickly. William Fanshawe was the largest of the local employers, and almost everybody in the neighbourhood either worked in his factories or was dependent upon somebody who did.

The day following the discovery of the body, one Jeremiah Cookson came forward and said that on his way home on the night of 4 November he had seen two children pushing what he took to be a Guy on a wheeled trolley. He had noticed them particularly because they were smartly dressed, and it seemed strange that two such children should be out alone at that time of night. It was well past midnight. So strange did it seem that he made a point of following them. They became aware of his footsteps behind them, and paused under a street lamp to look back. It was Robert and Muriel Fanshawe.

Cookson was a petty criminal, and the police were reluctant to rely on his evidence, but public opinion was pressing for an arrest. The creaking trolley, with its grotesquely masked burden, haunted the imagination. People had nightmares about it. What were the police doing?

Three days after the discovery of James's body the Fanshawe children were charged with James's murder and taken to Westgate Police Station for questioning. They denied everything and went on denying it. The great strength of their story was its simplicity. If they had been asked to account for their movements, or to supply alibis, they would almost certainly have begun to contradict themselves. But there was none of that. They were in bed, they were asleep, they knew nothing – and they said so over and over again. Their father, who, despite his grief, never wavered in his support for them, sat in on every interview. It was noticeable that during Muriel's interviews her father's gaze never left her face.

The first day of the trial dawned cold and bleak. People

hurrying towards the Moot Hall bent their heads to battle with the wind that blew off the Tyne, carrying with it flakes of stinging snow. The courtroom smelled of wet wool, and even at noon there was a constant hissing of gas jets.

Mr Justice Lowther presided. Muriel was represented by Patrick Johnstone, probably the best defence counsel of his day; Robert by the scarcely less distinguished Nigel Walters. Both children pleaded not guilty to murder.

Cookson, whose evidence was crucial to the prosecution, proved to be a bad witness. The children, when they paused under the street lamp, had been standing beside a wall. Were they shorter than the wall, Johnstone asked, level with it, or taller than it? About level, Cookson thought. Then it could not have been Robert and Muriel Fanshawe. The wall measured five foot ten inches. Muriel, the taller of the two children, was five foot three, now, and she had grown since then. How much had Cookson had to drink? 'A canny few,' Cookson said. 'A canny few,' Johnstone repeated. Mr Justice Lowther intervened to say he could attach no meaning to the word 'canny' in this context. As far as he was concerned, it meant shrewd, thrifty or explicable in natural terms. 'Were you the worse for drink?' he asked. 'No, my Lord, I was the better for it,' Cookson replied. (Laughter.)

His quip did Cookson little good. Johnstone established easily enough that he had been in three or four public houses that night and had consumed ten pints or more of strong beer. Worse than that, he had been dismissed from Fanshawe's works the previous year for drinking on the job. 'You have a grudge against William Fanshawe, haven't you?' Johnstone said. 'I know what I saw,' Cookson insisted. But he was becoming flustered, and Johnstone moved in for the kill, thundering across the courtroom: 'I put it to you that you saw what you wanted to see.'

It was apparent, even to those sitting in the courtroom at the time, that this was the pivotal moment of the trial. Proceedings dragged on for several more days, but it came as no surprise to anybody when the children were acquitted. The crowds who stood outside the courtroom as the Fanshawes left raised a weak cheer, but there were those who muttered, then and later, that money talked and that the Fanshawe children had got away with murder.

William Fanshawe never again spoke, or permitted anybody else to speak, of James's death in his presence.

Bad luck continued to dog the family. Isobel, whose health had never been good, did not long survive her son. Robert was killed on the first day of the Somme. One of his brother officers wrote to William Fanshawe saying that he had seen Robert's body impaled on the uncut German wire surrounded by unexploded British shells.

Muriel Fanshawe never married. On William's death,

Fleete House and the armaments factories, the bulk of his estate, passed to his nephew.

Robert's last letter to Muriel, written on the eve of his death, survives. In it, he describes the columns of marching men winding along the summer lanes, singing as they went; and of how, as they passed the huge pits that had been dug in the fields on either side of the road, ready to receive the dead, the singing would falter, and for a few hundred yards there would be silence except for the tramp of feet, and then, gradually, the singing would start again. He goes on to write of the universal hope that a decisive breakthrough might be achieved, and, with a frankness unusual in such letters, of his fears that the losses would prove extremely heavy. For himself, he says, he would not mind so very much, 'if it wasn't for the thought of leaving you with Father and the memory of James'. The next sentence is underlined so deeply that the pen has cut through the paper: <u>Remember how young we were</u>.

Muriel, by contrast, always insisted on her innocence. After her father's death she returned to Lob's Hill. No attempt had been made to sell the house and it was never let, but kept exactly as it had been when James was alive. Like Mary Ann Cotton, Muriel was used as a bogey-woman to frighten naughty children into obedience. The neighbours avoided her. When asked why she insisted on living in a place where she was regarded with so much suspicion, she replied that she would not be forced out. On the contrary, she intended to remain in Lob's Hill until the truth about 'that dreadful murder' was revealed.

It is always tempting to believe that a person who persistently maintains their innocence must indeed be innocent, but the reader may care to remember that, in the condemned cell at Durham gaol, Mary Ann Cotton wept bitterly because her mother could not visit her, though her failure to do so was entirely due to Mary Ann's having murdered her some years before.

We do not, and cannot, know what went on in the mind of the increasingly eccentric old lady who lived alone in the house that had once been her childhood home. People passing Lob's Hill along the lane behind the house would often see a light burning in the room with barred windows, the room that had been James's nursery: Muriel Fanshawe's apparently guilt-free memorial to a little boy who had always been afraid of the dark and whose first word had been 'sadda'.

The car-park's filled up since they arrived that morning. Rows and rows of cars, their windscreens and bumpers flashing in the sun, so many Nick feels disorientated, standing in the sparse blue shade of a pine tree, trying to remember where he's parked.

At last he sees the Volvo, in full sun now, though he'd left it in shade. Be like a microwave. Walking towards it, his shadow ravelling round his feet, he wonders whether he should tell Fran about the Fanshawe murder. Not to tell her seems patronizing, it goes against the whole grain of their relationship, but then he remembers the flood of tears that morning. She's exhausted, has been ever since the move, it would take very little more to push her over the edge. And he doesn't know how she'd react. This isn't just a sad old story; it happened in the rooms where they live and sleep and eat. The fact is nobody would knowingly buy a house in which a murder has been committed. You can tell yourself it doesn't matter, it's the past, it's over, but the fact is you wouldn't choose to do it. And Fran's pregnant. Now more than ever she needs to feel safe. It's not as if any useful purpose would be served by telling her . . . Later perhaps, when they've succeeded in stamping their own identity on the house. At the moment it still feels like a house-swap, with the actual owners expected back at any moment.

He opens the car boot, throws in the book, and, after a moment's thought, pulls a plastic bin bag over it. Right, that's settled, then.

People crowd round the circus tent, waiting for the next performance. No sign of Fran or the children. He walks towards the house and there, directly ahead of him, is Fran, strolling along towards the restaurant. He runs to catch up with her, and slips his arm around her waist. 'Where are the children?'

'Where've you been?'

'I went for a drink. Where are they?'

'I gave them some money for ice-creams. Did you get a guide?'

'No, they hadn't got any.'

Nick's looking at the ice-cream van. There's a short queue, but the children aren't in it.

'Are we going to eat here?' Fran asks.

'No, let's go to the coast, shall we? There might be a bit more of a breeze.'

The children aren't anywhere near the ice-cream van. 'I'll just see where they are,' he says casually, but then breaks into a run. Fran calls something after him, but he can't hear. He's panicking, telling himself not to be so bloody stupid, but there are so many streams and lakes round here, it's no place for a toddler to be on his own. But he's not on his own, he's with Gareth and Miranda. Nick's mind skitters away from the real source of his fears. He asks the man in the ice-cream van whether he's seen three children, a fair-haired toddler with an older boy and girl. A woman standing near by, swirling her tongue round an ice-cream cone, points to a path that leads down to the largest lake.

Nick careers down the hill, jumping on to the verge to avoid an elderly couple. The path's uneven, shelving down steeply between the roots of trees. A hundred feet below there's a stream, its water blackish brown, flowing over black rocks. Sometimes it flashes white over miniature waterfalls, or opens into deep pools with pebble promontories. Every hundred yards or so wooden bridges span the stream. There's a path on the other side too, narrower than this, bordered by glistening ferns that are almost as wet as the rocks. Nick crosses over and thinks he sees them, two taller figures holding a small boy by the hand. He opens his mouth to call their names, then realizes it's a couple with their child. His children are nowhere to be seen.

The fir trees tower over him. Even the roots are above his head. Only by craning his head back can he see glints of sunlight on the uppermost branches. A warm, dark, wet, enclosed place. It reminds him of the garden at Lob's Hill. All the trees and bushes are evergreens, their dead leaves forming a weed-killing mulch that kills everything else as well.

And then he sees them. Comes round a corner of the twisting path, and sees them, Jasper with his trainers and socks off, paddling; Miranda sitting on a rock sucking out the last drop of ice-cream from the bottom of the cone; Gareth standing on a rock in the middle of the stream, the turbulent water chafing round him.

Nick calls out, and all three children turn towards him, their faces pale in the gloom of the rhododendron bushes. They say nothing and he wonders what they see, what they make of him, this sweaty anxious adult who stands on the bridge above them, looking down.

NINE

After supper that evening, Fran and the kids settle down
to watch *Terminator 2: Judgement Day*. It's Gareth's favourite, he must've seen it twenty times, but he never gets
tired of it. Nick watches the opening scenes, and then,
as pieces of dead children begin to blow across the screen,
like leaves, in the nuclear wind, he retreats to the living
room and starts covering up the wall painting.

White paint. No time to worry about colour schemes,
he just wants the portrait covered. With a roller he draws
huge swathes of emulsion across the wall; the figures
disappear into a blizzard. Apple white, it says on the tin.
Alzheimer white.

Nick's shadow mimics his actions as he works. He's
the second person to do this. Fanshawe would never have
entrusted the cover-up to anybody else, his pride wouldn't
have let him. Now, for the second time, the faces sink
into the wall. He tries not to look at them, not to meet
their gaze. According to *Notable Northern Murders*, Muriel
always maintained that she knew nothing about how

James had died, but who, looking at this picture, would have believed her? And, judging from the age of the children, this must have been painted within weeks, or months, of his death.

He leaves James till last, then kneels down and applies the paint, with a small brush, in little dabs and darts. It's like washing Jasper's face, he half expects James to pull away. Now the eyes. He paints over them quickly, and then, still kneeling, feeling a complete fool, says, 'Night night.'

The rest of the wall can wait. He's just finished cleaning the roller and brush when the phone rings. 'I'll get it,' he shouts, not wanting the video watchers to be disturbed.

It's Auntie Frieda, shrieking into the phone – she's never really got the hang of them – saying she's been trying to get him all day.

'How is he?' Nick asks, expecting the worst.

'Home.'

'*Home?* He can't be.'

'He is.' She sounds elated and frightened. 'You know the consultant said he could come home next week, but I never thought they'd send him out on a Sunday. Need the beds, I suppose.'

'How did you get him back?'

'Oh, the ambulance took us.'

'How is he?'

'Tired. Look, he wants a word. Hang on a sec.'

A long pause. Sounds of shuffling steps and laboured

breathing coming closer. I should have taken them home by car, Nick thinks, torn again. If this drags on into October and the start of term there'll be no way he can cope.

A bump and a click as the phone's picked up.

'How do you feel?' Nick asks, speaking loudly, not because there's any doubt about Grandad's ability to hear, but because the telly's going full blast. He sticks a finger in one ear, and crouches over the phone.

'Fine. A lot better.'

'Does it hurt much?'

'Nips a bit. It'll settle down.'

'Have they given you anything for the pain?'

'I think the pink pills are for that.'

'Do they work?'

'Nah. I don't know where I am with them.'

Perhaps the dose is too high? Nobody knows what the right dose is for a man of 101. Geordie's walked off the end of the graph.

'Still, if they help the pain . . . '

'Nah, hot-water bottle's as good as anything.'

'Have you got one?'

'Frieda's bringing one up now.'

'Must be nice being in your own bed.'

'Champion.' He sounds exhausted. 'Look, I'm a bit bushed, son. I'll hand you back to Frieda, if you don't mind.'

Frieda shouts, 'Hello?'

'Is he really all right?'

'Oh, I think so.' Doubtfully.

'Do you want me to come over?'

'No, we're fine. Tell you what, why don't you come over for tea tomorrow? Bring Miranda. It'll do him good to have a bit of young company.'

'All right. You're sure you can manage tonight?'

'Why aye, man.'

He puts the phone down and goes to find Fran.

'Was that Frieda?'

'Yes, he's back home.'

'Already?'

'Yes.'

'Are you going across?'

'No, not tonight. She's asked me to go for tea to-morrow.' He doesn't know how to say that only he and Miranda are invited.

Gareth says, 'Ssh.' And for once Nick's glad of the interruption.

'Will you be taking Miranda?' Fran asks.

It's slipped in casually, one of those quietly lethal questions Barbara used to specialize in. Since no two women could be less alike, he's forced to conclude he's the type of man who inspires lethal questions. 'Yes.'

She nods.

'What'll you do?'

'Take Gareth shopping. He needs school shoes.'

She comes out on to the drive to say goodbye, a surprisingly fond farewell for so short a separation. Because the family's splitting into its constituent parts, they need to be gentle with each other. As she bends into the car to kiss him, he grasps her hand and she winces as the wedding ring bites. 'Don't wear yourself out,' he says.

Once they're on the road, Miranda stares out of the window at the passing fields, and Nick's grateful for the silence. He needs to prepare himself. The morning call from Frieda hadn't been reassuring. She was going to try to get some sleep, she said, while Grandad was watching cricket. 'How was the night?' Nick asked. A second's hesitation. 'A bit lively.'

Nick stops outside the house and sees, with a jolt of fear, that the curtains are drawn. Well, she's asleep, it means nothing. All the same he tells Miranda to stay in the car and tries the door. Locked. He rings the bell and a pink face blurred behind frosted glass surfaces to meet him. Frieda's voice: 'Who is it?'

'Me.'

She unlocks the door. Doesn't need to say anything, for there, framed in the open door of the living room, is Geordie, wrapped in a dressing-gown, watching television. Not dead, not yet, though Nick can see, even in the dim light reflected from the screen, that it won't be long. He's aged twenty years in the past week. Not in the sense of being more wrinkled or stooped, he's simply thinner. When he reaches up to receive Nick's hug his dressing-gown falls open and beneath the skin Nick sees, not merely ribs, but the beating of his heart. He's become a skeleton leaf. The merest breath of wind would blow him away, and yet he's still upright. Still the sunken eyes are clear.

'How's it going, Grandad?'

'Bloody awful. There's only Atherton in double figures.'

No way of telling whether the misunderstanding's genuine or whether he's simply determined not to talk.

'I meant, how are you feeling?'

'Not so bad. Got the stitches out.'

Almost boastfully, he pushes down his pyjama trousers to show the wound, wounds rather. Beside the bayonet wound, Shepherd's handiwork looks almost prissily neat. A surgical incision: nothing like this ancient scar, this relic of an attempt at gutting a human being. 'It's going on well, isn't it? Does it hurt?'

'A bit.' But it's the bayonet wound he's cradling in his hand.

'I've brought Miranda to see you.'

'Oh, good.'

Is it Nick's imagination, or is there a fractional hesitation, a shadow of doubt, as to who Miranda is?

'She must be nigh on fourteen, isn't she?'

It *is* Nick's imagination. Geordie knows exactly who she is.

'Where is she?' says Frieda. 'You've surely never left her in the car?'

He can't explain about the drawn curtains. 'I'll get her.'

Miranda comes in shyly, standing self-consciously by the china cabinet while they exclaim over her height. She's going to be a tall girl. Nick sees it more clearly now he's looking at her through their eyes, and for a moment he feels almost dizzy, wanting to slow the pace. He seems to be living in one of those speeded-up sequences beloved of wildlife photographers. Fran's stomach swelling, the children growing, the house rose blooming and decaying, Geordie dwindling into death before his eyes. Time must move at a constant pace, he supposes, but that's not how we experience it.

He waits until Miranda and Grandad are chatting, then goes into the kitchen to help with the tea.

'What pills is he taking?'

She gets them down from the shelf. 'Mr Shepherd says if the pain gets very bad he'll have to go back into hospital, but as long as he's OK he can stay at home.'

'Does he think it'll get bad?'

'No, he says quite often they just slip away.'

'Doesn't sound much like Geordie, does it?'

'No, it doesn't.' She stands twisting a pink striped tea towel round in hands that are as creased as tissue paper. 'I don't like to think about it.'

You'll have your life back, Nick thinks, but he can't

say that. There's too much he doesn't understand in this relationship. He knows that sometimes – no, often – Geordie and Frieda behave more like husband and wife than father and daughter. Not that he's suggesting – or thinking – anything wrong, but, emotionally, that's the truth. Just as when she forgets and refers to Grandad as 'your dad' that's also the truth. 'I'll carry the tray,' he says, and she holds open the door.

In the hospital Geordie had a beaker, but here he's reverted to his usual method of drinking tea, pouring a small amount into a saucer, blowing on it assiduously for several minutes, then raising the saucer to his lips. One of the recurring sights of Nick's childhood: an orange sea with the gale of grandfather's breath blowing across it. It had been a source of tension at home; Nick's father thought the habit utterly disgusting.

The saucer, precariously balanced, makes it all the way to Grandad's lips. He sips delicately, repeats the performance, and then he's had enough.

'I can't seem to keep tea on my stomach,' he explains apologetically, passing the saucer back. 'Fills me full of wind.'

Every twinge of pain – and in spite of all his disavowals it's quite clear from his braced position, his restlessness, that he *is* in pain – is firmly dismissed as 'wind'. An innocuous problem uniting the two ends of life.

The talk revolves round him, small circular talk about

family events, past and present, Miranda's school, what she wants to be when she grows up. On the screen men in white run up and down, or – more often – walk on and off, but silently. England are all out for a total that seems incredible. Geordie's eyes are closed, he doesn't notice or comment on the disaster. Abruptly he opens them and quotes with approval a tombstone he once read:

Let your wind go free
Where ere ye may be.
For 'twas the wind that killed me.

Never one to proffer advice he'd be afraid to follow, Geordie accompanies the quotation with an immensely long rumbling fart. Then he needs the toilet, urgently.

'It's like this,' Frieda explains to Miranda. 'He either can't go at all or he's got the runs. Never anything in between.'

As Geordie struggles to stand up, the front of his pyjama trousers gapes open, revealing a shrivelled cock, a dangling and wrinkled scrotum. Miranda blinks, but only once, and then she's helping Frieda wrap the dressing-gown round him, and offering her shoulder for him to lean on. But he prefers Nick's shoulder, he's tottery on his feet, needs more support than an old woman or a young girl can give. 'Bloody rations are late again,' he mutters, as they limp out of the room together. Or does he? A second later Nick isn't sure that this is what he heard. Probably not, since a second later Geordie makes, through the half-closed door of the lavatory, a disparaging comment on the England middle-order collapse.

The sight of Geordie's genitals disturbs him. It's not merely awkwardness about Miranda's presence, it's the speculation he doesn't want to have to entertain about what form sexuality might take in that inconceivably frail, and dauntless, body. How do you reconcile yourself to that loss? Sophocles was relieved. 'Like freedom after a life spent in bondage to a cruel master.' Sophocles was seventy. At seventy-eight Geordie had started an affair with Norah Atkinson, the widow of an insurance agent, a woman whose opulent bosom was frequently sheathed in Bri-nylon leopard skin. At home she'd gone down every bit as well as tea in saucers. Nick feels obscurely cheered by the thought of Grandad's 78-year-old cavortings. He starts to think how much longer his grandfather has had than his father, how much longer he's had than he might have had. Lucky to survive the bayonet wound. But even without that – Loos, the Somme, Passchendaele – the odds must always have been stacked high against his reaching twenty.

So Nick helps Geordie back into the living room feeling rather cheerful about the prospect of mortality, at least as it affected somebody else. Geordie too seems cheerful, doesn't talk much, perhaps, but the few comments he does make show he's following the conversation. As it grows dusk he remarks that the nights are drawing in. Part of him likes winter evenings, he likes coming in to a good fire. All the same he'll be glad when next summer comes. He dreads the ice and frost of January and February, and his tone of voice reveals no doubt that these are difficulties he expects to contend with. It's impossible to tell what he believes. They don't mention how ill he is. Perhaps he takes his cue from them and thinks he isn't? Equally likely he colludes with them for their sakes, the last dreadful courtesy the dying extend to the living. He can't last a month, Nick thinks, but he's no idea, really, how long a man of Geordie's formidable willpower might survive. At any rate it pleases him to see the old man with Miranda. He strokes her forearm, as if marvelling at the smooth flesh, and seems to take comfort from the contact. This is his great-granddaughter. He won't live to see her grow up, but he's lived long enough already to see the woman she will become clearly visible in the child.

After tea's cleared away and washed up, Nick takes Frieda to one side and asks if she wants him to come back that night. She hesitates, but he can see she's tired. 'I'll just take Miranda home,' he says. 'And then I'll be back.'

He rings Fran, but there's nobody there. Slightly puzzled – they ought to be back by now, Fran hates driving through the rush hour – he lets the phone go on ringing and ringing in the empty house, until finally the answering machine clicks on, and his own voice invites him to leave a message after the tone.

'Nobody in,' he says, going back into the living room to say goodbye.

TEN

Fran's car is so hot she has to open all the windows to cool it down before they can get in. She swings one door to and fro out of a vague feeling that this will help. Jasper's trying to throw handfuls of gravel, but his coordination's so poor he topples over and lands on his bottom. One whimper, and he's on his feet again, this time throwing the gravel at Gareth, who thumps him on the arm.

'Gareth!'

'He started it.'

'He's just a baby, he doesn't understand.'

'He started it.'

'Just get in, will you?'

Gareth sits in the front passenger seat.

'Not there. In the back.'

'Why?'

'Because it's the law. You're not allowed in the front till you're twelve.'

'Nick lets Miranda.'

'Miranda's thirteen.'

'I'm nearly twelve.'

'And when you are twelve then you can sit in the front.'

Gareth gets in the back. Fran's not inclined to congratulate herself. In dealing with Gareth, there's nothing more ominous than a small, early victory.

Jasper, who hates the hot plastic car seat, stiffens his legs till they're like planks. Fran, holding a heavy toddler at arm's length, back aching, stomach getting in the way of everything, pendulous breasts each with a swamp of sweat underneath, thinks, This is stupid. She stops, lets Jasper get out, and plays with him for a while, pretendy chases and tickling and incey-wincey-spider-climbed-up-the-spout, then when he's curled up and helpless with giggles she slips him quickly into the seat and clicks the buckle. He opens his mouth to scream, but she crashes the gears, turns the radio on full blast, starts to sing 'Incey Wincey Spider' at the top of her voice, until Jasper, bowling along the open road, breath snatched out of his mouth, deafened by the noise, forgets what he's crying about, and points at the shadows of leaves flickering across the roof. ''Ook, 'ook.'

'Yeah,' says Gareth sourly. ''Ook.'

Fran slips one hand into her blouse and surreptitiously rubs the sweat, flaps the cotton, does what she can to dry off. When she was a girl – back in the middle Jurassic – she'd been one of the last in her class to hold a pencil under them. Get pencil cases in there now. Be a pencil factory soon if she doesn't do something about this bloody saggy bra. 'Look, Gareth,' she says, trying to keep the lines of communication open. 'There's your new school.'

And why the fuck would anybody want to look at that? Gareth thinks.

But look at it he does. It's empty now, of course, the middle of August, a long, low huddle of buildings, one of them with its windows boarded up, because last winter the pipes burst and flooded the labs and there's no money to get them repaired. Though Digger says it wasn't burst pipes, it was his brother Paul and a gang of lads broke in and left the taps running. Gareth doesn't know whether to believe him or not.

He's dreading it. At his last school he knew all the places you could hide. Behind the fire escape, in the caretaker's cupboard, out on the flat roof, in the bogs. Gareth can make a pee last fifty minutes if he has to. And he knew all the boys. Who was hard, who wasn't, which of the girls was hard enough to take on nearly all the lads. Joanna Martin could take on everybody in 6M except Darryl Davies. There are 1,500 kids in the new school. He can't even imagine what it would look like, if they were all in a room together. Not that they ever are. You don't have assemblies in the big school. Instead every morning there's Family Groups, big kids, grown-ups, little kids all mixed up together. Like in families. It's supposed to make you feel safe and if Jasper doesn't stop saying ' 'Ook!' soon he's going to strangle the little fucker.

None of it would matter if him and Digger were still mates, because apart from anything else Paul always looked out for Digger – he might kick his head in, but he wouldn't let anybody else do it – only Digger hung round with Darryl and them now. When September comes nobody'll call for him. He'll have to walk up that drive on his own.

Last year was the best time. Digger and him had been a gang all on their own, people said you couldn't have a gang with just two, but you could, they were, though probably because nobody else wanted to join. And they made a den on the waste ground behind the railway line. A stream ran through it, with lots of willow trees, small ones, and they always had rags and bits of polythene hanging from the branches. At one point the stream had big pipes going across it, making a kind of bridge, and then on one side it opened out into a swamp and further up there was a steep hill with bushes on the top. Gareth saw you could have a den in the bushes, they were quite thick, nobody'd be able to see in. But what was even better you could dam the stream, flood the marshy ground and turn the whole area into a real bog, like in the *Hound of the Baskervilles*, and nobody'd know the way through, but they would, and anybody who tried to find the den would sink into the mud with screams and yells, hands clawing and waving in the air until there were just a few bubbles breaking on the surface and the hands sticking out, twitching a bit, and then going still and sliding slowly into the mud. Fucking brilliant.

But the marsh wasn't easy to flood. He was the one who saw how to do it, nobody else, but by that time they'd turned into a real gang, everybody wanted to join. Even Paul sort of belonged and one night the three of them slept out and Paul spunked up. He said he had and Gareth didn't disbelieve him for a second because he went all red in the face and there was a new smell in the tent.

He didn't know why it had gone wrong. Except they all started thieving and one day in Woolies Gareth panicked and ran away and Darryl got nicked and blamed him though it wasn't his fault and Darryl said he was chicken and Digger joined in and then Darryl started pushing and shoving and trying to make Gareth fight and there was a ring of lads all round yelling and Digger was yelling and when Gareth got knocked over and kicked in the teeth he didn't do anything, didn't even say anything. Just looked.

'Can I go to Metroland?' he asks.

'After we get the shoes.'

And after I find somewhere to park, Fran thinks. Round and round, up and down, why couldn't people stay at home and sunbathe? She'd never expected it to be this busy. She sees a place, on the edge of the road in full sun, but it'll have to do. Jasper stands patiently while she gets her handbag from under the passenger seat and then puts his hand in hers. 'All right, off we go.'

Gareth's dragging his feet, not just figuratively. 'It's no wonder your shoes don't last,' Fran says, as he scuffs and trails along behind.

The windows of clothes and shoe shops display huge photographs of smiling children, neatly dressed in school uniforms, clutching new pencil cases and satchels, greeting the new term full of energy and hope and youthful vigour.

Twats, Gareth thinks.

Mum stops outside Stead & Simpson. 'All right,' she says. 'Let's have a look in here.'

The next hour's a nightmare. It's the sort of thing you'd like to blot out of your consciousness for ever, but you can't. Fran was afraid, when they set off, that Gareth might be uncooperative, but it's worse than that. He's being pseudo-cooperative. Every shoe in the shop's on the floor in front of them. Gareth's still limping obediently up and down. 'No, it's too tight,' he says, shaking his head regretfully. 'Would you like to try the other one?' says the assistant. 'What's the point of trying the other one if this one's too tight?' Gareth snaps. Mask slipped a bit there. He forces a smile.

'No good, I'm afraid,' the assistant says to Fran. She wants them out of the shop. Jasper, excited by the idea of taking shoes out of boxes – he's been watching her do it for an hour – decides to join in. Soon high-heeled shoes from the ladies' display stand are flying through the air. It's time to retreat.

Outside Fran says to Gareth, 'If you ever show me up like that again, I'll bloody murder you.'

'What have I done? It was him hoying shoes.'

Fran walks on.

'But of course that's all right, isn't it, he never gets wrong for anything.'

'He's a baby. He doesn't understand.'

'Anyway they don't wear shoes like that.'

'Black shoes, Gareth. It says on the list.'

'I know what it *says*. But they *wear* trainers.'

He can't understand why she doesn't get it. If he goes to school wearing shoes like that he'll get filled in. And then he thinks, What does it matter? He'll get filled in anyway.

Barratt's next. Jasper can't believe his luck, and immediately starts following the lady round, taking shoes off the stands and hurling them across the floor with shrieks of joy. Fran, desperate, taps him on the leg, not hard, but he starts to scream. Several women turn to stare at her. Rotten lousy mother, she hears them thinking. Can't control her child without resorting to slaps. 'No, it rubs a bit at the back,' she hears Gareth saying. Dragging a screaming Jasper by the arm, Fran marches across and says, 'We'll take those.'

By the time she gets them out of the shop Jasper's

dancing with rage. Fran kneels down and tries to reason with him. Several women turn to stare at her. Stupid, middle-class, Hampstead-style mother, she hears them thinking. Can't she see what that child needs is a good slap?

And then Gareth starts, and that's terrible because a two-year-old having a temper tantrum's just normal. An eleven-year-old boy having one's a case for family therapy. She offers him money to go to Metroland, too much money, she's bribing him, she knows she is, she doesn't care, and then, guiltily relieved to see the back of him, takes Jasper into Mothercare. He's quiet now, upstaged by Gareth's performance, by how much sheer noise Gareth can make.

Twenty minutes later Fran's in a communal changing room trying on shirts, about the only garment she can get into now that will still fit her after the birth. The room's crowded, but at least Fran's spared the usual feelings of inadequacy. She has a cast-iron excuse for having no waist. Jasper's sitting on the bench staring at a little girl, a few feet away, who's sucking her thumb and watching her mother try on dresses. That's what I could do with, Fran thinks. A bit of mother–daughter bonding. 'What do you think?' the mother says, craning round to see her back view in the mirror.

The little girl takes her thumb out of her mouth, and says, 'Your bum's wobbly.'

The woman and Fran exchange glances and laugh.

Cancel the mother–daughter bonding, Fran thinks. I'll settle for a football team.

Five minutes later Jasper's near the end of his tether, grizzling and pulling his ears. Fran pays, scrabbling about for her Access card, and in the process drops all her bags. Blowing wisps of hair out of her eyes, she picks them up again, but by this time Jasper's run out of the shop. She chases him, grabs him by the hand, pulls him, screaming, back to the counter, collects her things together again, forgets the blouse, goes back, gets it, finally sets off for Metroland, where she finds Gareth absorbed in a game that involves too vaguely oriental-looking gentlemen taking it in turns to kick each other in the head.

'Come on, Gareth.'

'Aw, Ma-am.'

'No, look, Gareth, come on. If we go now we can get a video. You can choose it.'

For a moment it looks as if she's in for another temper tantrum – he hasn't been this bad for a long time – but then, with a final tap and pull of levers, Gareth gives in. Laden with bags, Jasper running on ahead, Gareth trailing behind, Fran trudges to the car and reaches for her keys. No keys. No handbag. *Christ*. Where can she have left it? For a few moments her mind isn't blank, it's a jumble. She sees herself on a bank of video surveillance screens going into half a dozen shops at once. All those shops, but no, wait a minute, she had the bag just now in the dress shop. She had to scrabble about in the bottom to find the Access card. Oh, Christ, the Access card. All her credit cards, car keys, cheque book, house keys.

'I've left my bag,' she tells Gareth, dumping all the carrier bags in front of the bumper. 'You stay here with Jasper.' She's already running, stiff-legged and clumsy, across the car-park, calling over her shoulder as she goes, 'Don't move.'

Gareth sits down with his back against the bumper. Jasper stares at Fran's back, runs a few steps after her, but she's going too fast and soon the glass doors swallow her. He starts to whimper. 'Want Mummy.'

'Well, you can't have her, so shurrup.' Gareth reaches for the bag that contains his school shoes, and lifts the lid. They nestle in white tissue paper, big, black, shiny, like bombs. And they make school real. He's been pretending it won't happen, but it will. He closes his eyes and Darryl's face floats on the inside of his lids, all the faces, the ring of faces crowding in, looking down at him on the floor, jeering, and the iron taste of the blood in his mouth.

A car's horn beeps. Gareth opens his eyes, and Jasper's standing in front of a car, it's had to stop for him and the driver's leaning out. 'Come on,' Gareth says, picking him up and carrying him, awkwardly, because Jasper's a lot heavier than he looks. He keeps kicking, and screaming, 'Want Mummy.' 'Shurrup, man,' Gareth says, and then suddenly he's fed up. Screeching little brat, he never has to do anything he doesn't want to do, if he falls over it's oh never mind Mummy kiss it better, and the driver's yelling at *him*. Gareth waits till he's sure he's not being observed, then drops Jasper on to the ground. 'There, you've bloody well got something to cry about now, haven't you?' There's a graze on Jasper's forehead with three dark beads of blood. 'Chicken,' Gareth jeers, watching him scream. And then he kicks him.

A minute later Fran comes running back, smiling all over her face, so she must have got the handbag. 'Oh, never mind, baby,' she says, bending down. 'Did naughty Mummy go and leave you?' She sees the graze.

'He fell over,' Gareth says.

'Weren't you watching him?'

'He ran after you.'

There's something here Fran doesn't like, but she knows she won't get to the bottom of it, you never do, and anyway it's her fault, as always. She shouldn't have left them. 'All right. Get in the car.'

When Jasper's finally in bed and asleep Fran kneels and watches him for a while. There's a little catch in his breath now and again, the ghost of the hiccupy sobs that eventually, on the drive back, made him vomit. She'd had to stop in a lay-by to clean him up.

Gareth ran upstairs as soon as they got back, more sobs, this time behind closed doors, and then the familiar *flit* of laser guns.

She could do with a drink, but she won't have one,

of course. She hasn't had a drink since the second blue line came up on the pregnancy test. Instead she changes into a loose nightdress and lies down on the bed with all the windows open.

Gareth. Is it abnormal for an eleven-year-old to have temper tantrums in a shopping mall? Probably. No, not probably – it is. If she tells Nick he'll only say what he always says, that they should take Gareth back to see Ms Rowe. Ms Rowe of the snake hips and tits pointing at the ceiling. Who might just possibly pop out one designer baby when she's thirty-eight and it's least likely to bugger up her brilliant career. Ms Rowe is Fran's enemy. Fran doesn't trust her, because she says Gareth has a marked tendency to bully younger children, and that's always going to make him difficult to contain in a mainstream school. Fran pointed out that he was going to secondary school in September, and there wouldn't be any younger children. That took the wind out of her sails a bit. Had there been problems at home? Ms Rowe asked. No, Fran said very loudly. I expect that's because he's expressing it all at school, Ms Rowe said. You can't win with these people.

Meanwhile she'd better get up and get the tea ready. Gareth must have crept downstairs, because by the time she's made ham sandwiches he's in the living room watching *Terminator 2* again. She puts his sandwich and a bag of crisps beside him, and joins him on the sofa. Sarah Connor's watching her son teach the Terminator to do high fives, while she reflects, voice over, that of all the would-be fathers who'd come and gone over the years, this machine was the only one that measured up. In an insane world, it was the only sane choice.

Gareth's father was a stain on the sheets. The first three prospective stepfathers weren't much use either. Not that Gareth gave any of them a chance. He hasn't had so much as a birthday card from his father in all these years, and yet he rejects all substitutes. What is it he's being loyal to? Ultimately, it must be to his own DNA, to the part of his genetic make-up that doesn't derive from her. There's nothing else, it really is as impersonal as that. He won't have Nick at any price.

She thinks how unhappy he looks with his skinny arms and legs and the bloody awful number 2 cut he insists on. He's got a hand in front of his face and might just possibly be sucking his thumb.

He catches her watching him. 'What's the best bit, do you think?' she asks.

He takes his hand away and the thumb is wet. 'The bit where he says, "Hasta la vista, baby" and blows the guy away.' A companionable silence. 'Which do you think's the best?'

Fran selects at random. 'Oh, the bit where the baddie Terminator melts down and you think he's gone and then all the little bits come together again.'

'Yeah, that's good too.'

They watch to the end. As soon as it's over he jumps

up and presses buttons, then comes back and sits closer. She runs her fingers through the stubbly hair and he doesn't pull away. If only he was like this all the time, he does have a good side, he sometimes sees she's tired and makes her a cup of tea. He just doesn't seem able to cope with other children.

She puts her arm round his shoulder and they sit in silence, listening to the whirr of the rewinding tape.

ELEVEN

'Poor little scrap,' Nick says, bending over Jasper's cot. 'You have been in the wars.' Already, beneath the superficial graze, there's an area of darkened skin. 'It's going to be a nasty bruise.'

Fran comes across to look. 'Do you think I should call the doctor?'

'No, I don't think so. He's been all right since, hasn't he?'

'Fine. I'll take him into the surgery tomorrow.'

They go downstairs to the kitchen, where Nick pours himself a whisky and Fran a Perrier. 'How was shopping?'

'Horrendous.'

'But you got the shoes?'

'We got the shoes. Which leaves the shirts, the trousers, the tie, the gym kit and the blazer.'

'You know, I think he might be right about the blazer. You don't see many kids wearing them.'

'That's what it says on the list.'

'No, but you remember university, first day you buy

the college scarf, second day you chuck it in the bin – might be a bit like that.'

No, Fran thinks, I don't remember university. I don't remember how it feels to have a waist or a decent night's sleep or a pee without somebody yelling and banging on the door. I don't remember *life*.

Then she thinks, snap out of it, you frigging miserable cow. A gin would help. Nick offers her one; she has a second Perrier with ice and lemon instead. 'How was Geordie?'

'Not good. In fact, I've said I'll go back tonight. He's very restless.'

'Can't they give him sleeping pills?'

'They have, he won't take them.'

Silence.

'I know it's a lot to ask.'

'No, it's not. It's just . . . Miranda.'

'I thought she might help.'

'I can't use her as a nanny. Anyway, she's got her own problems.'

'He's not going to last more than a week.'

'All right.' She leans across and kisses him. 'Ring me before you go to bed?'

Geordie's face becomes more skull-like as night approaches. It's just the effect of increasing tiredness – Nick knows that – but it's difficult not to imagine that he's witnessing flesh peeling back from bones, revealing what's been there all along, working its way to the surface from the moment of birth. Geordie nods off, then wakes with a start, staring round him as if he doesn't recognize the room he's in. With darkness falling, the other world closes in.

At nine thirty, immediately after the news, he says, 'Well, that's it, then, I'm done in.'

Nick goes upstairs with him and sees him settled into bed. 'There's nowt like it,' he says. 'Nowt like your own bed.' He burrows down on the left-hand side of the double bed. Even after forty-odd years he still leaves space for his wife. With part of his mind he's convinced she's just popped across the landing for a pee.

Geordie falls asleep immediately, and again wakes, this time with a cry of fear. Nothing, it's nothing. The room comes back. Some old bugger's sitting up in bed blinking at him; after a fractional hesitation he identifies his reflection in the mirror. There's sweat in the creases of his neck. It's always so vivid, Harry's face clearer than his own hand in front of his eyes, and yet distorted. Harry disappears, bit by bit, like the Cheshire cat, until only the screaming mouth is left. Night after night he feels himself falling towards that mouth.

Nick pops his head round the door. 'I thought you were awake. Do you want to come back down?'

'No, I'll stop up here. She's a good-hearted lass, Frieda, but she'd wear any bugger out.'

Nick goes downstairs to find Frieda wrestling with the

mysteries of the video recorder. 'Morecambe and Wise,' she says, wheezing from the exertion. 'Won't do your Grandad any harm if we have a laugh.'

Upstairs Geordie, dozing with half-closed eyes, hears the laughter and thinks, Sounds like a good show. He's floating on the edge of darkness, a pale square just in front of his eyes that looks like a window but can't be because there aren't any windows here. After a while he feels the chicken wire creak as somebody sits down beside him, and lies, tense and still, seeing only a dark shape. 'Harry?'

'It's me, Grandad.'

Bloody cheek, calling him Grandad, whoever it is. A light's switched on. Geordie blinks at the roses on the wall, at the strange face bending over him, a face that gradually becomes familiar. 'Nick.'

Nick, seeing he's dazzled by the lamp, reaches for the switch.

'No, leave it on a bit.'

It helps, Nick sees, to locate himself in a brightly lit room. Darkness, by disorienting him in space, loosens his grip on time as well.

'Has she gone home?'

'Who?' Nick asks, testing for confusion.

'The cat's grandmother.'

'Yes. Is there anything I can get you?'

'No, I've got me water. I'll be right.'

But he shows no sign of settling down. They're in for

a bad night, Nick thinks. Night's being turned into day, the upside-down time of the trenches, funk holes by day, working parties and patrols at night. Geordie's living to the tick of a different clock.

Nick puts his feet up on the sofa, not ready for bed yet. He's brought the transcripts of Helen and Geordie's tape-recorded conversations with him, and dips into them at random as he finishes his drink.

To begin with Grandad didn't understand what Helen was after. He was used to people asking questions about the First World War, but Helen's mainly interested in afterwards, not in the content of his memories but in how he coped with them later on. There's comparatively little about the war itself, and perhaps this is why there's no account of Harry's death. It's not the only reason, though. Geordie sounds uncomfortable whenever Harry's mentioned.

HELEN: What was Harry like?
GEORDIE: Oh, he was a grand lad. Into
      everything, you know, played football, sang in
      the choir, amateur dramatics, all that sort of
      thing, anything really, if there was owt going
      on he was in the thick of it. All the lasses
      chased after him, and me mam, well, she
      absolutely idolized him.
HELEN: And you hero-worshipped him?
GEORDIE: Did I hell. (Laughs.) I was jealous to

death of him. I remember when we were lads we used to swim in the river and there was a bridge you could jump off and the water was quite deep. Harry would have it I was too little, so I had to guard the clothes, and I remember watching our Harry jump in, waiting for the bubbles coming up, you know, and I used to think, Go on, you bastard, drown. And then when he come up I used to think, Thank God. (Laughs.)

HELEN: You joined up at the same time as Harry?

GEORDIE: Yes.

HELEN: And you were in the same regiment?

GEORDIE: Yes.

HELEN: He was killed in 1916. Did you ever wonder why it was him and not you?

GEORDIE: You always wondered that. One time there was six of us by the side of the road and I'd ate something that didn't agree with me. I just had to do a runner fast as I could. I was squatting down with me trousers round me ankles when a shell come over and they'd gone. You see you can't make sense of that, can you? I got the squitters, so I'm alive. Where's the sense in that?

HELEN: What were their names?

GEORDIE: Harry Parks. Joe Hardcastle. Douglas Horn. Billy Watson. Walter Baines.

HELEN: When did it happen?
GEORDIE: August 31st 1915.

That's typical of the clarity of his memories. He remembers everything, talks about everything – except Harry. Helen gets back to the main thread of the interviews, or what she intends to be the main thread.

HELEN: What sort of state were you in when you got back?
GEORDIE: When I came back?

For Nick this is one of the chilling moments in the transcripts. There's something curiously blank about that repetition of her question, almost as if he's wondering whether he did come back.
The silence worries him. He hurries to fill it.

GEORDIE: Pretty bad, I suppose. Nine pence to the shilling, I suppose you'd say, but I wasn't the only one, there was a lot like that.
HELEN: You got over the bayonet wound all right?
GEORDIE: Never bothered me. Aches a bit when there's rain coming. It's a better weather forecaster than them buggers on the telly, I tell you that.
HELEN: So it was your nerves that were bad?

GEORDIE: Yes, nightmares, I used to wake up shouting. And I had an awful stammer. I suppose the truth is I was shell-shocked, but they didn't seem to talk about that in them days. You just had to shut up and get on with it. You know, you were alive, you had the same number of arms and legs you set off with so what the bloody hell were you moaning on about? That was the attitude, and for all you were supposed to be heroes and all that you didn't have to say much before they accused you of malingering. You just had to snap back. Knicker elastic, that's what we were.

HELEN: And you couldn't?

GEORDIE: No, well, I couldn't. I think with me only being eighteen, well seventeen, when I joined up I'd never really got established, you know. I think mebbe some of the older lads with jobs and kiddies, and all that, there was like . . . You know, they had something to build on.

HELEN: You were twenty-one when you came back?

GEORDIE: Yes.

HELEN: An old twenty-one?

GEORDIE: In some ways. No experience of anything that mattered. Job? I knew how to kill people. Not a lot of demand for that. And it's

not much use when it comes to chatting up the
lasses either.

HELEN: I can't believe you ever had any problems
with that, Geordie.

GEORDIE: Didn't know where to start, love. I
do now, but it's not a lot of use to me *now*, is
it?

They flirt outrageously, these two. No wonder Geordie
always wore a suit for the interviews. A clean shirt, a tie.
Would spread newspaper on the kitchen table the night
before and clean his shoes.

GEORDIE: Me mam never got over our Harry,
and that was the root of a lot of my troubles.
Wrong one died, simple as that.

HELEN: Are you sure that's what she thought?

GEORDIE: She said it. At our Harry's memorial
service, she turned round to me as we were
leaving the church, and she says, 'It should have
been you.'

HELEN: She came right out and said it?

GEORDIE: Oh yes.

Helen doesn't believe this. Nick knows, because she's
told him so. She's heard the same story seven or eight
times from other veterans. It isn't that she thinks he's
lying, either to himself or to her, but she believes he's

remembering a communal myth rather than a personal experience.

Nick doesn't know what to think. It's possible Helen's right, but then isn't it equally possible that the same incident happened seven or eight or a hundred times to different people? The country must have been full of grief-stricken women wishing somebody else had died, and too far gone in misery and bitterness to hide the truth.

HELEN: And that still hurts?

But Geordie's not having any of that. The question's answered by silence.

GEORDIE: She got into spiritualism, me mam.
    Well a lot of the women did – and a few men.
    And there was this chap who used to take
    photos of people who'd lost somebody – a son
    or a husband or whatever – and lo and behold
    when the picture came out there was the
    person they'd lost in the photograph with
    them. So what could you do? Me mam was set
    on it and so Dad and me and our Mary all got
    our glad rags on, and off we went. The Great
    Family Portrait. I don't know what I expected,
    I couldn't see any fraud going on, but then it
    wouldn't be done then, would it? Anyway,

when we got them there was this, I don't know, *thing*, in the background. You couldn't make out the features, but you could just about see it was a face. And me mam says, 'Oh, there's our Harry,' and she bust out crying and, I don't know why, but it absolutely knocked my end in, did that. I was no good at all after.

HELEN: When was that?

GEORDIE: 1919. When the Armistice come on, you know, I didn't want anything to do with that. I knew I couldn't go through with it, the parades and all that, so I went to the coast instead. I walked miles and I didn't have me watch on me so I didn't know when it was eleven o'clock. But I was silent all day anyway, so it didn't matter.

HELEN: Did you go to subsequent parades?

GEORDIE: Only once. I know a lot of men found it helped them, but I just, I just couldn't, I just didn't want to be reminded. The only time I did go was because little Geoffrey – our Harry's lad – was going to be in it, and I felt I had to. But even then, I wished I hadn't. There's this little lad standing there with Harry's medals on his chest and he didn't know what the hell it was about. All he knew was he was going to get jelly and custard afterwards. They always gave the war orphans a slap-up tea in the Scout

Hut. And afterwards I heard him boasting to his pal about it, and this other little lad turns round and he says, 'I'd rather have me dad.' Oh, and the look on Geoffrey's face. Do you know, up to that time, I don't think he'd made the connection between having no dad and stuffing his face on all this jelly and custard. You could see on his face, it was a real blow. I didn't hold in with all that, anyway. Cubs and Boy Scouts wearing their dads' medals and marching.

HELEN: Did you think there was an element of glorifying war in it?

GEORDIE: To an extent I did, yes. That and the hypocrisy. There was men fought in that war who were struggling to keep a roof over their family's heads. If you must know, I used to think some people remembered the dead so they could forget the living with a clear conscience.

HELEN: You thought –

GEORDIE: I thought we'd been conned, love. (Laughs.) I *knew* we'd been conned.

HELEN: You didn't find it easy to get work?

GEORDIE: Tramped round for two years before I got anything, and then it was in a scrapyard. I lived in a shed in the yard, and I had this little dog, a Jackie Russell it was, I loved that dog. Well, I was earning a living, but I was, I don't

know, on the fringes, I suppose. They were all
saying in our street, Geordie's a tinker. Me
mam was mortified. Oh, it was a disgrace, that
shed. She come up one afternoon with our
Mary and of course the place was spotless.
Didn't matter, it was still a disgrace. And then
about that time I palled up with these lads, and
we used to go to the Palais, big bunch of us,
and I'd have a dance with the lasses. You
needed a lass to dance with in them days. These
days they just stand up on their own and
wriggle. But after the dance was over I never
tried talking to the lass, I just used to take her
straight back to her mates and more or less
dump her.

HELEN: Why?

GEORDIE: Stammer. I didn't tell you about the
stutter did I? Paralytic, couldn't get a word out.

HELEN: Doesn't seem to bother you now.

GEORDIE: No, but it did then. You know I was a
good dancer, I wasn't bad-looking, no, no, I'm
not being vain, I didn't say I was good-looking,
I says I wasn't bad, but as soon as I opened my
mouth that was it. You'd see the poor lass
thinking, Oh, heck, what have we got here?
But then I got on with our lass.

HELEN: And she was different?

GEORDIE: Oh yes, totally different. And it wasn't

easy for her, she had a helluva job with me
when we were first married, because I was still
having the nightmares and I used to wake up
screaming, but it was worse than that. You
know, I should be ashamed to say it, I suppose,
but I used to wet meself. She'd wake up and
there I'd be, screaming and clawing at the wall,
and the bed'd be drenched and she'd be
drenched. There's many and many a woman
wouldn't've put up with what she did, and do
you know she never once threw it up at me?
She used to sit on the bed beside me and get
hold of me hands and she used to sing:

> Keep yor feet still, Geordie hinny,
> Let's be happy for the neet,
> For we may not be sae happy thro' the day,
> So give us that bit comfort,
> Keep yor feet still, Geordie lad!
> And dinnet drive me bonny dreams away.

She was a good woman. She died forty-five
years ago, and I can truthfully say there hasn't
been a day gone by that I haven't missed her.

HELEN: And then you got a job?
GEORDIE: I got took on at a printer's. I loved
that job, all these b's and c's I couldn't say, I'd

just pick them up and slot them in. Click, click. Magic.

HELEN: You were happy?

GEORDIE: I was very happy. Still am. I've got nothing to complain about, I've had a good life.

HELEN: But you still didn't go on the parades or anything like that?

GEORDIE: No, but I remembered in me own way. Every August 31st I'd say the lads' names over to meself, and there were other dates as well. June 22nd.

HELEN: Harry?

GEORDIE: Yes. Harry.

A rare reference to Harry's death, not pursued. All Geordie's words, Nick realizes suddenly – and there are thousands of them in this interview alone – orbit round a central silence, a dark star. And yet his nightmares, now, are not about 'the war'. They're about Harry. It's Harry's name he shouts out in the night.

Before he gets into bed Nick winds up the clock Grandad keeps on the table in the hall, then takes it into the living room and closes the door on it. He'll still hear the chimes, but as long as he doesn't fall into the trap of listening for the next quarter it shouldn't disturb him too much. We have heard the chimes at midnight, Master Shallow . . . Grandad certainly has, more often than most.

Nick stops to listen outside Geordie's door. The mattress creaks, a few gabbled words, then silence. He goes into the spare room and opens the window. The moon's just rising above the trees. Long shadows leap across the backyard wall and reach for the house. He gets between the sheets and turns off the light.

It's the dead still of night when Nick wakes and lies, half dazed, awaiting the repetition of the sound that woke him. Silence. He's settling himself to sleep again, thinking that after all it must have been the chimes of the clock that disturbed him, when he feels a current of cool air move across his face. A window's open, or a door. He gets up and looks out, sees nothing, but then he hears the rattle of the latch on the back door. He races downstairs to the kitchen, but it's empty. Light glares from the naked bulb; the room looks surprised and desolate. The back door's wide open and Grandad's standing at the bottom of the yard, arms clasping his skinny chest, staring at the sky. Wisps of cloud chase each other across the moon. Geordie's a column of slippery light and shade; grey and silver shadows net his white hair. Nick calls his name, but he doesn't turn round.

No time to find coat or shoes. A light rain's been falling, the sloping, green-algae-coated surface of the yard feels greasy under his toes. Geordie sees him coming, his fingers find the latch, the door opens and he's gone. Nick follows him out into the alley. The ground's cobbled, the cobbles silver-edged and distinct in the moonlight, rounded as skulls. Geordie's got halfway along the wall. He's staggering, bent almost double, but then, as Nick watches, he crouches, listens, moves on again. Nick wants to cry with the despair of it. Geordie's reached a telegraph pole, and hides behind it. Nick begins to creep along the wall behind him, not wanting to shout his name and wake the street, still less to chase after him and add to the terror he must be feeling.

He's got to within a few yards, dodging the piles of dog shit that litter the alley, when Geordie with the agility of a much younger man sinks to his knees and starts slithering across the cobbles on his elbows and knees, pausing, waiting, lowering his face to the ground, edging forward again. Nick edges closer. He hears Geordie muttering to himself, but then he moves on again, making for the wood. But which wood is it? Devil's Wood, High Wood, Mametz, Thiepval? Geordie crawls faster, slithering away into the shadow of the trees.

Nick's grasp on the situation starts to slip. His day-time self, the sane sensible middle-aged man coping as best he can with a confused elderly relative, vanishes. It's too insubstantial an identity to survive in the dark wood at night. He forces himself to cough, a harsh sound that has Geordie spinning round. No trace of recognition. Nick goes up to him. He looks entirely mad, striking Nick flat-handed over his head and shoulders as Nick tries to get hold of him. Nick bats him off with blocking movements of his raised arms. Geordie's blows are slow, exhausted and clumsy. He's floundering like a man in mud or fire.

All this has been silent, but now Geordie starts to yell with rage. Lights go on all along the row of houses, so that their slow scufflings are illuminated in overlapping orange squares. Curtains are pulled aside, pale faces look down, realize it's not a burglar, not a threat to them or their property, and half withdraw behind the shelter of closed curtains.

The lights and faces where no lights and faces should be reduce Geordie to a quivering abject terror, horrible to see. Nick can't take any more. 'Grandad,' he says. 'Come on now, come back to bed.'

Grandad. The preposterous word. Geordie peers at him, at the middle-aged, unknown face. He looks across the lane at the sharp angles of roofs, dark against a blanching sky; and not the horrors of the past, but the incomprehensibility of the present makes him afraid. He starts to shake, as on those night-time slithers through the wire he never shook, only trembled slightly, stomach muscles clenching, a sickness of anticipation rather than of fear.

'Grandad,' the stranger says again.

Geordie looks down at himself, at the pyjama jacket, the fuzz of white hair on his chest, and starts to cry. Nick puts his arm round him, cradling the whiskery cheek in the fingers of his other hand, and begins half pulling, half dragging him towards the house. Geordie struggles again as they reach the yard door.

'Look,' Nick says, groping for words that will make sense in both worlds. 'We've got to get back, it's nearly light.'

Grandad scans the sky, sees dawn massing grey clouds edged with gold, and lets himself be helped back, limping barefoot over the cobbles.

In the kitchen Nick examines him. He stinks to high heaven and can't be allowed to get back between the sheets like that. It's not the dirt, it's the dog shit. Nick takes off his pyjamas, and puts Grandad's own mac round his shoulders. He sits on a high stool, while Nick lays a towel on the floor and gets to work washing his feet, his head nudging Geordie's bony knees as he works. When the feet are clean, he dries them on the towel, and then scrapes the mess off his stomach, aware all the time that he's doing this to a dying man, that Geordie's life is ebbing away as he sits upright, God knows how, on the stool.

'Do you want a fag?'

Geordie turns his head in the direction of the voice, and his lips move. Nick lights one for each of them, puts Geordie's between his lips, and drags deeply on his own. Geordie's concentrating on his first draw. He sits, silent, inhaling deeply, a blue mist between himself and the world. Are they in the trenches now, a dugout in the front line perhaps, or are they in the back kitchen of 22

North Road? Nick doesn't know. Wherever Geordie is, he's there too.

Nick leans against the wall, which sags alarmingly under his weight. None of the attempts to repair the plaster over the years has ever worked. This is it, he thinks, not confused, not even tired any more, just seeing clearly. He never talked. All through Nick's childhood Grandad had said nothing. His body with its ancient wound, as hard to decipher as the carving on a rune stone, had been left to speak for him. Over the past twenty years, the time he should have been dead, he's talked endlessly, delivering his stark and simple warning, but now they've come full circle. There he is again, silent, under the wreath of smoke.

'Come on,' Nick says, tossing his cigarette into the sink. 'Let's get you to bed.'

They go upstairs – a jostling of uncoordinated hips and shoulders in the too narrow space – and then on to the bed, where they collapse, panting like lovers.

'Come on now,' Nick says. He pulls the sheets further back, lifts Grandad's scaly shins off the floor and into bed.

'I can't, I've got to –'

'No, you haven't,' Nick said firmly. 'There's nothing you've got to do.'

He switches on the lamp beside the bed, thinking it might be reassuring for Geordie to see the familiar room, but he looks round at the furniture in bewilderment and then, in real terror, at Nick's face.

He doesn't know who I am, Nick thinks. There's a moment of narcissistic pain, of real diminishment. For the first time in his life he looks into the steel mirror and it doesn't reflect his face. More important things than that to think about. Geordie's cold. 'Do you want a bottle?'

No answer. Nick changes out of his filthy pyjamas, fetches a clean T-shirt and pants, puts them on and gets in beside him. They'll get warm, probably, sooner or later, though he doubts if he'll be able to sleep. The window's a square of definite light. He lies, tensely, aware of the other body, reluctant to turn and look at him. He wonders whether Grandad's remembered who he is.

Time passes, he doesn't know how long, or whether he's been to sleep after all.

Geordie's eyes are wide open. He mutters something and Nick bends closer to listen. He can't make head nor tail of it, except that it's about Harry.

'What about him?'

No reply. After a few minutes Geordie's breathing slows and Nick risks a sideways glance. At first he thinks he's asleep, the eyes are white slits in his grey face and his mouth's fallen open. But then the tip of a purple tongue appears and runs round the pale lips. He says, and the words cling to his dry mouth, 'I killed Harry.'

Nick turns towards him. It's not true of course, it's obviously a delusion, but there's no denying the reality of his despair. He grasps his cold hand, but, after a few moments, Geordie wriggles his fingers and gently, almost apologetically, takes the hand away.

TWELVE

Next morning, standing in the kitchen with his hands clasped round a cup of coffee while Frieda unpacks her shopping bag, Nick's able to imagine he's back in childhood. The events of last night are blurred with sleep. Geordie's in the living room, talking about what he wants for his breakfast. He looks forward to meals eagerly, though he never eats much. He can't be bothered to go all the way upstairs again, he says, so he gets washed stripped off at the kitchen sink, and this too produces a flood of memories, for Geordie always washed like that at the kitchen sink, bluthering and spluthering the soap around his face, digging powerfully into his ears with his fingertips, his face emerging blind and pink from behind the towel. Off to the working men's club, usually. Not to the British Legion – when Nick was growing up he'd still been avoiding that. Always wore a buttonhole when he was going out, a yellow rose or a carnation. Replaced once a year, without comment, by a poppy that appeared and disappeared.

Nick goes into the living room and sits on the arm of the sofa, while Grandad chases his food around the plate, saying, 'Nice bit of bacon, this,' though most of the nice bit of bacon's still on the plate when eventually he stops pretending and pushes the tray away. He lies with his hands pressed against the swell of his stomach, clasping the bulge from the sides. Many of his gestures echo Fran's. Life growing inside one belly; death in the other. A banal reflection, Nick thinks, ashamed he can't push his thoughts beyond the banal. The truth is he's just too bloody tired. The supply of emotion's run out.

Before he leaves he rings Helen and arranges to meet her outside the University library at ten o'clock. She's waiting for him under the sin tree, where student smokers go to smoke, sitting quietly on the low stone wall. He bends down and kisses her.

'How is he?'

'Pretty bad.' Now that he's away from the house, Nick's more aware of how deeply last night had shaken him. He sits beside her on the wall, hands dangling between his knees. 'He said he killed Harry.'

Her expression doesn't change.

'I wondered if he'd said anything to you?'

'Harry wasn't his favourite topic.'

'No, I noticed that. Couldn't change the subject fast enough, could he?'

'What exactly did he say?'

'Just that. "I killed Harry."'

'What sort of state was he in?'

'When he said it? Confused, frightened. He'd been wandering about half the night, on patrol. I got him back to bed – he obviously didn't know who the hell I was – switched the light out. I thought he'd gone to sleep, and then – no warning – out of the blue – "I killed Harry."' Nick can't stop himself sounding aggressive, as if this is her fault. 'I'm sorry, it's –'

'What do you want me to say, Nick?'

'O-oh, that he's reshaping his memories to fit in with current myths and assumptions about the war?' His smile fades. 'I want you to tell me it didn't happen.'

'I can't tell you that.'

'Or anything else either?'

'It was off the record. I promised I'd destroy the tape.'

'And did you?'

'Yes.'

'I just want to know whether I'm dealing with a senile delusion or –?'

'Or what?'

'You tell me.'

'If it is a delusion, it's still his reality.'

'Yes, but it doesn't have to be mine. For God's sake, Helen, I spent part of last night crawling on my hands and knees across bloody No Man's Land.'

Load of pretentious crap, he thinks a second later. He'd been nowhere of the sort.

Helen says, 'Why don't you ask him?'

'All right,' he says, standing up. 'I will.'

'Have you time for a coffee?'

'No, I'd better be getting back.'

She nods. As he walks back to his car, he calls over his shoulder, 'I don't believe you destroyed the tape.'

On the drive back he's chasing possibilities round and round his mind. Everything from a persistent delusion sparked off by survivor's guilt to actual murder. What better place for that than on the Somme? Though he doesn't believe it for a second, he knows Geordie too well.

Fran's just setting off for the shops when he gets back, and hands Jasper over to him with relief.

'You been a bad lad?' Nick asks, nuzzling his neck. Jasper smiles shyly and hides his face.

'No, he's all right,' says Fran. 'It's Gareth, I don't know what's got into him.'

The shoe box lies in the back of the cupboard, old sweaters piled on top of it, out of sight, buried.

But Gareth knows it's there. It's a bit like *Raiders of the Lost Ark* when the Ark's in the hold of the ship and everybody's laughing and talking, but then it starts humming and burns a hole in the crate. Gareth wouldn't mind if the shoes burnt a hole in the box; be even better if the box burnt a hole in the shoes.

At the back of the cupboard, there's a carrier bag full of old toys, soldiers, Action Men, Robocops,

Terminators. He doesn't play with them any more – though there is one he still likes. A clockwork sniper: you wind him up and he crawls across the floor. If you lie with your cheek pressed against the carpet he looks like a real soldier, because you can't see how small he is.

Gareth rolls on to his back and looks at the ceiling. Eleven days to the start of term. For weeks he's been telling himself it won't happen. In the middle of August it seems possible the school holidays will last for ever. But then suddenly it's nearly September and the days disappear like water down a plug hole. He sees himself, the same size as the sniper, whirling round in the current, shouting, drowning, nobody looking, nobody listening.

Because it's intolerable to be on his own, he goes down to the kitchen and mooches about there. Nick's still not back, his grandad's ill or something. For the millionth time, Mum says, 'Why don't you go out and play?' And for the millionth time he opens his mouth to say, 'We don't "*play*".' Only there is no 'we'. He closes his mouth, and revolves round the kitchen, turning round and round along the wall, dislodging spoons and skewers and fish slices as he whirls. He knows he's doing it, he knows it's terrible, he can't stop. He revolves up the stairs and through the hall till he gets to the front door, where he stops, breathless and dizzy. Mum's followed him, but she just stands there looking angry and frightened, so he has to go out just to spite her.

He decides to go to the school, and makes himself run

all the way there. It's raining, it's been raining all night, part of the running track outside the school's flooded. The drive must be a mile long, it's much longer than it looked from the car, and eleven days from now he's going to have to walk up it. With two tanks on his feet.

Gripping the railings, he feels trickles of wet run down his wrists and under his sleeves. When he takes his hands away his palms are crossed by broad pink bands with white ridges on either side. He splits a flake of rust with his thumbnail. 'You're getting it out of proportion,' Mum says. 'You'll enjoy it once you're there.'

He knows more about things than Mum does, some things anyway. About this estate for a start, about the kids who nick off from school and shove petrol-soaked rags through the letter-boxes of empty houses and drop matches on them. And then they call the fire brigade and stone them, and when the police come out to protect the firemen they stone the police too. Mum doesn't like him walking through the estate, because she knows about the gangs, but when she talks about the school it's, 'Oh, you'll soon make friends.' Where does she think the kids at school come from? They're not being bussed in from Mars.

He'll go home that way, across the estate. If he has to come to this school, he might as well start getting used to it.

The streets are deserted. Too early for the kids: they come out later, streaming across the waste land, past the burnt-out cars, past the charred houses, to the recce or the chippie or the wall outside the pub. There's glass on the road, shiny like a river. He crunches through it, looking at his feet. And that's why he doesn't see the kid till he's almost on top of him. He's playing on a sort of trolley thing, going 'broom broom' like Jasper does. Dead cool now, zero cool, Gareth drawls out of the corner of his mouth, 'Hasta la vista, baby,' and kicks him.

Then he looks up. A girl's standing on the base of the next lamp-post, frozen in the act of swinging round it. She's got a white top on that shows her tits, though she's only about twelve, and she's looking at him with a sort of slow anger. She's in no hurry about this, she's enjoying it. It's the sort of feeling Gareth knows well, like when you want to shit and you won't let yourself. Behind her are three more girls, but they're waiting for her to do something first, because this kid's her brother.

Gareth knows the worst thing he can do now is to look frightened. He daren't turn and run. She lets him get level before pushing her clenched fist into his chest. 'So what's he done to you?'

It sounds entirely reasonable, but it isn't. He can see the excitement on her face and on the faces of the other girls crowding in behind her. They watch him go past, but it's just like cats letting a mouse escape, as soon as he's gone a few yards they start following him. He walks faster. They walk faster. He runs, they run. Two at the front, the big fat slag and the little one who's skinnier though still bigger than him. He darts down an alley between the houses and realizes he's trapped himself, because it's harder to run here, the cobbles are slippery, he skids and nearly falls and then they've got him. 'What do you want?' he says when he feels the first girl's hand on his anorak. He hasn't got any money, if he had he'd throw it at them and run. 'Show us what you've got,' the fat lass says. 'I haven't got any,' he says. He only realizes what they mean when they shriek with laughter. He tries to run, but they're on to him, dragging at his shorts, and he's fighting them. Clutching, clawing, trying to keep himself covered up. The skinny one punches him in the guts and when he bends the fat one knees him in the face, and he lets go of the shorts. He can't look, his eyes are streaming, he keeps them tight shut, but he knows from the feel of the air on his skin that they can see everything.

'What do y' call that?'

'Jesus Christ, I've seen bigger on a budgie.'

'You want to watch a bird doesn't see that.'

'Ooh, look, at him, Jackie-no-balls.'

He feels the shorts pulled further down, and doesn't resist because nothing worse can happen now.

'Skid marks!'

It's true. He sees it himself, the brown streak in his pants, as he pulls the shorts up.

'Skid marks! Skid marks!' they shout after him, as he runs crying down the alley and out into the street.

The strange thing is that though they soon stop following him, he can still hear them shouting, even when he's running up the drive and into the house.

They'll go to the same school, they're the same age as him, a year older perhaps. Even if they don't know where he lives they can easily find out. He wonders why he was ever bothered about wearing the wrong shoes because this is fifty, a hundred times worse, and all the time inside his head there's a voice shouting, 'Skid marks! Skid marks!'

THIRTEEN

Miranda lies on the lawn at the back of the house, sunbathing and listening to her Walkman. She sees herself, long and pale, with big sunglasses that look like insects' eyes.

A cloud moves over the sun. The shadow starts at her feet and moves upwards, chilling her body inch by inch, until at last the orange glow behind her closed lids dies to a dull purple. She opens her eyes and watches the shadow creep over the garden, encroach on the terrace until it reaches the house and every rose is quenched.

The night Dad left, the house was full of bangs and shouts and screams and slammed doors. Then silence. Miranda stood covering her face with her hands in a corner, then, when she couldn't bear it any longer, ran across the landing to Mum and Dad's room. Dad had a suitcase open on the bed and his back was turned. She crept round the door, not knowing whether she was wanted or not. As soon as he saw her, he picked her up and hugged her tight enough to hurt. And then she looked over his shoulder and saw his suits and shirts and ties in the case, and a row of socks rolled up in pairs, all along one side, like a litter of dead puppies.

Dad said to her once, 'You know, I wouldn't blame you if you were angry.'

But she's not angry. She's never angry.

Dad calls, 'Miranda?'

They must be nearly ready to leave. Reluctantly, she gets up and goes back into the house to find the usual chaos of preparations well advanced.

'Miranda?' Fran says. 'Could you go into the living room and get Jasper's bye-bye? I think it's in there.'

His bye-bye's a yellow blanket with a satin binding that he stuffs into his mouth and strokes whenever he's tired. Most of the time he just ignores it, but if it's missing when he wants to have a nap all hell's let loose. She's sick of fetching and carrying after Jasper, but she doesn't say anything. Fran's got Jasper *and* Gareth to cope with, and half the time Dad's not here. It's no wonder she grabs every bit of help she can get.

Miranda goes into the living room. It's bright sun outside and the blinds are half closed, making a pattern of yellow and black wasp stripes on the floor, but she sees the bye-bye straight away, draped over the back of a chair. She's just stretched out her hand to pick it up when she realizes she's not alone.

There's a girl at the french windows, shielding her eyes to peer through the slats of the blinds into the room. If it had been a man Miranda would probably have screamed, but because it's a girl she's not frightened. Though there is something horrible about this girl, the way she moves up and down along the window, scanning the room, her movements quick and eager, like a stoat outside a rabbit's cage.

Miranda takes in very little about her appearance. Partly the blind obscures her, partly Miranda's almost too shocked to register anything. She takes one step towards the window, intending to challenge her, then, realizing it's locked, tears out of the room and races down the side of the house on to the terrace. Quick as she is, the girl's gone before she gets there. She must have gone through the side entrance out into the road, though by the time Miranda opens the gate she's already turned the corner, and there's nobody in sight.

Miranda returns to the terrace and, on some obscure impulse, presses her own face against the window, peering into the room with shielded eyes, trying to see what the girl saw.

The door opens and Jasper comes trotting in – he's probably decided to get his bye-bye himself. He runs towards it and then, exactly as she'd done herself, seems to realize he's not alone. He raises his eyes to the figure on the other side of the glass, gazing in at him, and screams and screams and screams.

Miranda steps back, feeling as guilty as if she'd frightened him deliberately, then walks round into the house.

Fran's got there first, scooping Jasper up into her arms, where he sobs and clutches his bye-bye.

'What happened to you?' Fran asks.

'There was a girl at the window.'

Gareth's on to it at once. 'What sort of girl?'

Miranda shrugs, furious with herself for mentioning it, because now Gareth'll say she's afraid of ghosts, like he did the night they found the painting. 'Just a girl. I chased her, she ran away.'

'How old?'

'Twelve. Thirteen.'

'Fat?'

'I don't know, Gareth. I only got a glimpse.'

She was wearing a long skirt, and her hair was long, but that doesn't mean she was a ghost. A lot of girls wear long skirts, some of the time; nearly all the girls in Miranda's class have long hair, including Miranda. She's not going to say any more, because Gareth'll only twist it. Though he doesn't look capable of twisting anything at the moment. He's so white you'd think he was car sick and they haven't even started yet.

Two hours later, after Sunday lunch in a pub, they're trudging across a car-park with the sun on their backs.

'Are we going home now?' Gareth asks.

'No,' Fran says. 'We're going to the seaside.'

Fran's got prickly heat on the backs of her thighs, Nick's shirt has sweat moons in the armpits. It takes them ten minutes to get Jasper into his seat. Gareth walks up and down the car-park, kicking an ice-cream carton. They're always so patient – it never seems to occur to them to give the little bugger a good slap. When he's finally strapped in, wailing, miserable, red in the face, pulling at his ears, Gareth slides in beside him. The plastic glues itself to the backs of his thighs. He winds the window further down and looks out, wincing at the glitter of sunlight on bumpers and windscreens.

They have to queue to get out on to the main road. Jasper cries. Miranda sits hunched up, ignoring Jasper, who flails his fists and hits her repeatedly on her bare arm. Whenever this happens, she gives a sickly smile. She always pretends to like Jasper – another reason why Gareth can't stand her. He stares at her tits – not as big as the fat slag's, but you can still see them. Once the car gets going on the main road and there's air blowing through, Gareth shuts his eyes and forgets about her and Jasper.

That girl Miranda saw must have been the BFS, as he's started to call her – Big Fat Slag. She's found out where he lives.

He opens his eyes and sees tall fields of wheat on either side of the car. Further away there's a field of stubble, with those big shredded-wheat shapes scattered all over it. Jasper's gone to sleep. He pongs. When they get to wherever they're going Mum'll have to change him. Miranda's been sunbathing in the garden for the past week, though her skin's the wrong sort of skin, anybody can see that. It just turns pink and flakes. She's scraping a tiny flake of skin off her shoulder now.

'Don't do that,' Mum says automatically, catching sight of her in the mirror. 'I'll put some cream on it when we get there.'

Miranda flushes and doesn't say anything. Gareth looks at her sideways, thinking she's only two years older than he is and it's stupid of her to pretend to be grown up, though she does it all the time, she thinks she can get away with it. He used to be able to frighten her, but now he can't. She just smiles in a sort of tired way, like Nick, or gives him a long considering stare. He's never liked her, but not being able to get at her any more makes him feel lonely.

The car goes over a bump. Jasper wakes suddenly and starts to cry. Mum twists round in her seat with a bottle of water in her hand and tries to reach his mouth, but the seat belt digs into the bulge, she can't get anywhere near him. 'You give it to him, Gareth.'

'Do I have to?'

'Well, it wouldn't hurt you,' Nick snaps.

Gareth looks up and sees Nick watching him in the mirror. He takes the bottle. Jasper's lips shoot out towards it, he's so eager, like a sea anemone, wet and pink and disgusting.

'Tilt the bottle more,' Mum says. 'You'll give him wind.'

'I'll do it,' says Miranda, angling the bottle properly so

the area behind the teat fills with water. Jasper's mouth slackens, his eyes flicker upwards like a doll's. Gareth aims a kick at Miranda's shins, misses, hits the back of Nick's seat.

'Do you mind? I'm trying to drive.'

As if being the driver gives him a licence to be bad-tempered. He's always more horrible in the car than anywhere else.

They're just turning into another car-park. Nick drives up and down the aisles looking for a space. Gareth sees Mum notice one, open her mouth to point it out and shut it again. Nick hates backseat drivers. Gareth hates everybody. He doesn't see why you have to have families at all. It'd be much better if people just spawned like frogs.

This is a place they often come to. Once you leave the car-park and walk across the road to the beach, there are miles and miles of pale sands, with the sea a narrow brilliant line far out, and grass waving on the tops of the sand dunes. Further along there are cliffs.

Gareth fidgets while Mum changes Jasper on the back seat, and Nick fumes because he's fed up with it all, and Miranda mooches about four or five car lengths away, not talking to anybody, and Gareth suddenly thinks, Suppose somebody sees me? It's true nobody's likely to see him, but suppose somebody did? Walking down to the beach with a little boy and a bucket and spade. They might think he was going to make sand castles. And

Miranda. Somebody might think she's his girlfriend. Gareth goes hot and cold with the horror of it, and starts walking along the path, ahead of the rest of the family, trying to look as if he isn't with them.

Mum and Nick sit down in a sheltered part of the sand dunes. Mum'll go to sleep straight away, she always does these days. And Nick'll pretend to read the paper, but really he'll go to sleep too and Jasper'll play with his bucket and spade. And batty Miranda'll just wander about. He's got to get away from them as fast as possible; he's got to make it clear he's not part of it.

The path from the sand dunes to the beach winds down among huge blocks of concrete. Tank traps – 'dragon's teeth' – left over from the last war. Some of them are buried in the sand, with only three or four inches showing above ground. When he first came here, he was only a year or two older than Jasper, and jumping along the line of dragon's teeth had been a triumph. Not that they were very far apart, but the sand was fine and silky and every surface you landed on was slippy.

Further along the beach, where winter storms have eroded the shore, there are the massive blocks that stand out uncompromisingly square and bleak. Narrow slits of machine-gun emplacements look out over the shelving sands towards the sea. When Gareth was little he used to like playing in them, though you nearly always hurt yourself, clambering over the rocks that choked the entrance, and even when you got inside there were only chip cartons, beer cans, a smell of piss. Condoms too, though he didn't know what they were then. He picked one up once and ran back with it to Gran, trying to blow it up because he thought it was a balloon. Gran nearly had a fit.

He stands on the beach now, barefoot, with the waves creaming over his feet, feeling how much older he is, inclined to be contemptuous of his younger self. Behind him are the slit eyes of the bunkers and he feels sand slip beneath his toes, the land squirming away into the sea, as the tide pulls back. When the tide's right out, even further than it is now, it uncovers rock pools, and you can find things in them, little grey-green crabs hiding under the seaweed. He liked making them do things, switching them from pool to pool, or marooning them far up the beach and watching them try to crawl back. You squat down and look into the pool and it's a bit like *Jurassic Park* – you're like a dinosaur looking through a car window at the helpless squealing wriggling pink kids inside.

He wants to be with the others, it's not much fun on your own. He wades back through the sea, knee-deep, it's easier than struggling through the sand. It might look as if he's paddling, but he isn't, he's just walking with his feet in the water.

They've moved closer to the sea. Mum and Miranda are building a sand castle with a large moat round it, though they're wasting their time, anybody can see the tide's going out. Jasper's fascinated. He wants to help, but when he tries, patting the top of a turret, it collapses and Miranda has to start again.

'Just let him pat the bottom of the bucket,' Mum says.

Miranda does as she's told. Jasper squeals with delight.

'I'll get some ice-cream,' Nick says. 'Cornets everybody?'

He strides away up the beach. Gareth knows he'll take a few minutes sitting on the sea wall, having a quiet smoke before he comes back. Might even sneak off for a pint, it's been known.

Gareth finds an empty coke can, half buries it in the sand, about thirty feet from where they're sitting, and starts lobbing stones at it.

'Mind Jasper,' Mum says.

He's nowhere near bloody Jasper. Suddenly angry, he kicks sand in the direction of Miranda, who stops what she's doing and looks up through the tangle of her hair. Something about her expression startles him. He understands suddenly that if Miranda did what she wanted she'd knock the sand castle over and jump up and down on the ruin. She'd scream and shout and kick sand into all their faces. She doesn't say anything, she doesn't do anything, but then she never does, only he sees her wanting to, and he backs away. She's no right to feel like that. He's the one who wants to smash things.

'If you can't play properly,' Mum says, 'just go away.'

Play. That just about sums it up. All at once the eyes are back, clustering on his head and neck. Look at Gareth playing sand-pies with his baby brother.

He turns away from Mum's accusing look, Jasper's stupid blue-eyed stare, Miranda's sudden unexpected ferocity, and starts walking along the sand towards the cliffs.

'What about your ice-cream?' Mum calls after him.

'Don't want it.'

He keeps his head down, doesn't look back.

The cliffs have warning notices with pictures of falling rock. He doesn't care. He looks up, squinting into the sun, which is still fierce, and sees how, at the top of the cliffs, grass stems score the sky and seagulls soar far above with sunlight on their wings.

Cutting into the cliffs there's a deep ravine, lined with wet ferns and mosses; a brown stream meanders between mossy stones out over the beach and down towards the sea.

Gareth starts to climb, clinging to the ferns, stepping from ledge to ledge, his feet wet on slippery stones. As he climbs higher the moss and fern give way to clumps of bleached grass, dry and pale as straw. He catches hold of a clump and stifles a cry of surprise as the grass cuts him. There's a smear of blood on his palm which he squeezes to make more, then sucks away.

Further along a gull watches him with shameless naked amber eyes. He flaps his hand at it, and reluctantly, heavily, it takes off, sweeping down towards the beach, so that he sees its back and its stretched-out wings, darker than the underside, and he's almost dizzy with the thought that he's above the gulls. They're flying below him.

The sound of the waves turning over on the shore comes more faintly here. The seagulls mew and yelp. He feels like one of them, crouched on the narrow ledge, with his legs dangling over the edge. It's safe enough, as long as you keep still. But he's surprised himself, climbing as far up as this. It's not the sort of thing he usually does, and it opens a sort of door in his mind. If he can do this he can do anything.

He watches Nick carrying the ice-creams back to the family, stepping cautiously, the cornets clasped in his hands, looking down at them. He looks so small, so insect-like, toiling over the vast expanse of white, that Gareth feels superior. He doesn't know I'm here, he thinks. He doesn't know I'm watching him. And he feels a wriggle of excitement in his stomach. He leans forward and drops a pebble over the edge, watching it bounce once, twice, on jutting-out bits of rock before it hits the beach. They're all eating ice-creams. He doesn't care. When they're finished he sees Mum and Nick lie down side by side, Nick's arm thrown across her. Miranda wanders off towards the town. Jasper's playing with his sand castle, blundering about, knocking it down.

Cautiously Gareth looks up at the top of the cliff, wondering if he could climb all the way up. But craning up at the blue-white sky makes him dizzy. He clutches the rocks on either side of him, but they crumble in his hands, and he feels more frightened than if he hadn't tried to hang on to anything. He presses himself back against the cliff face, feeling sick and dizzy, knowing he's gone pale. It's nothing. After a while he's able to look down again. It's funny, looking up makes him go dizzy and looking down doesn't.

He closes his eyes, feeling the cliff wall against the back of his head, and immediately a voice says in his ears 'Skid marks!' It's like he's turned into a Mama doll; except when he closes his eyes the voice doesn't say 'Mama'. That'll be his nickname all the time now. As long as he goes to that school, and everybody who hears it for the first time'll say, Why's he called that? And she'll tell them, the big fat ugly stupid slag'll just fucking tell them. He wishes she was dead. He wishes he could kill her, but it wouldn't be any use just killing her, he'd have to kill them all. He can't even remember how many there were. He just hears the voices. Skid marks! Skid marks! Skid marks!

Miranda's disappeared behind the dragon's teeth now, Mum and Nick lie stretched out on the sand. Nick's taken his shirt off and folded his arms on his chest like a crusader knight except that his feet aren't crossed. Mum's resting her hands on her stomach like she always does. Her face is broad and blind, obviously asleep. With Nick you can't tell, but Gareth thinks he must be asleep too, he lies so still.

Jasper goes and stands over them, nudging Mum's arm. When she doesn't move he stands for a bit longer and Gareth can tell by the way his face screws up that he's nearly crying.

Jasper squats down in the sand a little way from Mummy and Daddy, poking about with a lolly stick. The sand's hard and damp here. Further up, where Mummy and Daddy are, it's pale and silky. When you go from this bit to that bit you get the other sort of sand stuck to your feet. There's another lolly stick further on, and when he gets that one there's another, and he sees a castle with lots of lolly sticks on top.

Jasper's wandered away from Mum and Nick now, he's coming towards the cliff. He looks very small and pink, trotting along, like a piglet. It's funny he doesn't know Gareth's there. Every now and then he stops and picks something up. At first Gareth can't see what it is, but then realizes Jasper's collecting lolly sticks. As he gets closer Gareth hears him chuntering to himself, the way he usually does when he's playing. Doesn't make sense.

The sun's mercilessly hot against the cliff face. There's no escape, no shadow. Jasper's shadow's like a black rag fluttering round his feet. He's coming towards the cleft in the rocks where the stream is. Gareth nearly calls out, but then decides he won't. It's more fun watching what Jasper does, without being seen.

Jasper's trying to throw the lolly sticks into the stream — he wants them to be boats — only his idea of throwing's to put both arms behind his head and bring them forwards together. He doesn't know when to let go, so either the lolly stick lands on the ground at his feet because he's held on to it too long, or it drops behind him because he's let go too soon. He does it again now and topples over. He's not hurt, but he cries anyway and then when Mum doesn't come running he stops and tries again. This time he gets the stick into the stream and squats on his shadow, watching it bob along. Then he gets tiny little pebbles and throws them at the stick. Now he's got his boat he wants to sink it. Gareth leans forward to see what he's doing and in the process sends a small stone skittering down the cliff face, starting a little avalanche of other stones as it falls. Jasper looks round – too late, and in the wrong direction – but bombing the lolly boat's too fascinating and he quickly goes back to that.

Gareth keeps very quiet and still while Jasper's looking round, searching. The sun's hurting his eyes, he feels sick. Part of him wants to join Jasper by the stream, to show him how to sail the boats, they could have a whole fleet and sink the lot, but something, some desire to spite even himself, makes him stay where he is. He's sweating all over. Sweat stings his eyelids, he closes them for a moment and immediately the voices start. Skid marks! Skid marks!

Further along the beach, Fran mutters in her sleep, Nick turns towards her, but doesn't wake.

★

Gareth claws up a handful of small stones and starts throwing them into the water, Plop, plop, plop. The plops attract Jasper's attention, he keeps turning, but never in the right direction. He doesn't have the sense to work out where the stone's coming from. It's like playing with an ant, it's so easy to make him do stupid things. The stones start to get bigger, make bigger plops. Jasper's nearly spinning round, looking first one way, then another, but never up at the cliff. Gareth throws faster, reaching for stones and clumps of hard earth at random, but he's not doing anything wrong because he's not aiming at Jasper, he's throwing to miss.

Suddenly the back of his neck feels as if he's being watched. Pressure. He looks up and sees Miranda on the cliff above him. The grass and her skirt and hair are all waving in the wind. She must have seen him, but she says nothing, just stands there, black against the brilliant sky. He can't see her face. He waits for her to speak, she must have seen him throwing stones, but she doesn't say anything. He turns, his tongue huge and dry in his mouth, and throws again.

Jasper looks up, sees the bright air turn solid and black and hard and come hurtling towards him. A flash of sunlight reveals a dark figure on the cliff and then his head bursts open, explodes in pain and wetness, and he falls backwards, water rushing in at his mouth and nose, blood in his eyes and on his tongue.

He comes up again, hair plastered to his skull, T-shirt

draped in green slime. He doesn't look like Jasper now, he's crying and his head's bleeding and Gareth's terrified of him, terrified of what he's done, so terrified it's easier to go on than to go back. He feels Miranda behind him, not speaking, watching, and throws again. He didn't mean this. The stone catches Jasper on the side of his head, knocks him over and yet still he gets up. He's got to make him stay down, stop crying, stop making that awful noise. He picks up a bigger stone, draws back his arm to throw again, but Jasper's screaming has woken Fran.

She's standing up, shouting 'Jasper?' at the top of her voice. Nick's on his feet too, dazed with sleep, running blindly in the direction of the screams. Gareth puts the stone down, sees Jasper lying among the rocks, bleeding, then turns carefully and starts climbing down, hand over hand, holding on to clumps of grass. Once he stops and looks up, but there's nobody on the path.

Nick runs faster than Mum, so gets to Jasper first. Gareth stands by the stream, smelling the cool dank smells, and watching Mum stumble across the pebbly sand and catch the wet bloody body into her arms.

They don't look like real people, Gareth thinks, they look like actors on the telly. Their mouths open and shut but either no sound's coming out or he can't hear it. Water and blood from Jasper's head make a big pink patch on Mum's dress just above the bulge. When the sound comes back it comes in a burst, hurting his ears.

Nobody asks him what happened, but he tells them anyway. 'He slipped, he slipped and hit his head on the rocks. I told him they were slippy.'

But they're not listening, they're too busy trying to decide what's best to do. Jasper's crying. There's a lot of blood, it's in his eyes, he looks awful. Nick probes the cut and says, 'It'll need stitches.'

Gareth doesn't understand this. He can't understand why Jasper's crying. From the moment the first stone hit his head Gareth's known he was dead. He was dead already after the first stone, it's just that he wouldn't lie down. He'd thrown the other stones out of despair because he wouldn't stay down. He'd wanted it to be over quickly.

'We need something to press on it,' Nick says. 'Gareth, can we have your T-shirt?'

He pulls it off and watches them press it against Jasper's head. Red spreads all over the white, it takes no time at all. Gareth hugs himself, shaking in the heat, his arms goose-pimply, his nipples little wizened currants.

Miranda appears from somewhere – not down the cliff – and they all walk back to the car. Nick wants to run, Gareth can see him wanting to, but he goes slowly and steadily, and on the T-shirt wrapped around Jasper's head the red goes on golloping up the white. In the car-park people cluster round, asking questions, giving advice, but nobody can do anything.

They get into the car, Mum sits in the back with Jasper,

192

Miranda in the front and at last Nick can go fast. They turn out of the car-park and on to the road in a spray of gravel, and nobody nags Gareth about fastening his seat belt as they generally do.

He looks at Miranda, but she won't look back.

FOURTEEN

Outside the casualty department there's a notice that says: AMBULANCES ONLY PAST THIS POINT. Mum gets out with Jasper, who's stopped crying but looks very white. He's been sick, there's a yellow patch on Mum's dress now as well as blood. 'I'll be as quick as I can,' Nick says.

They find somewhere to park. It's not difficult, there's a space just round the corner. Nick pulls on the hand-brake. The car smells of sick. Three nurses walk past in stripy dresses and black lace-up shoes.

'Do you want to come in?' Nick says. 'Yes,' says Miranda. And Gareth says he does too, because it might look peculiar if he didn't, and anyway he doesn't want to be alone.

Jasper's in a small room with a number on the door. Number four. Miranda and Gareth sit on plastic chairs in the waiting room and pretend to look at magazines. They're facing each other. Once Gareth looks up and sees Miranda staring at him. A long hard cool stare.

She'd seen everything. She knows Jasper didn't fall, she's just waiting for the right moment to tell.

Gareth sits stiffly on the plastic chair, no longer pretending to look at the magazines. He puts his hands under the backs of his legs and his skin feels strange against his skin. He waits for them to come out and tell him that Jasper's dead.

When he can't bear waiting any more he gets up and walks along the corridor to Room Four. The door's open. Jasper's sitting up on a trolley in the bright light with dried blood all over his face, a thick stream of new blood moving sluggishly over it. Mum pushes the tacky hair off his forehead, Jasper's whimpering, Mum's nearly whimpering as well. Nick sits on a chair, his hands clasped between his knees, looking as if he wants to kill somebody. Nobody's saying anything.

Gareth goes back to the waiting room and sits down again. Miranda looks up from her magazine, licks her finger slowly, and turns a page. After a while Nick comes out, kneels down in front of Gareth and says it's very important for Gareth to try to remember whether Jasper lost consciousness. 'Did he look as if he was asleep?'

'No, he didn't,' Gareth says, and his voice sounds weird, it's so long since he used it. 'He started crying as soon as he fell down.' He feels Miranda's eyes on the side of his face.

Nick goes away. Five minutes later he comes out again with Jasper on a trolley. A porter's pushing the trolley and Mum's walking on one side and Nick on the other, and there's a nurse in a navy-blue dress walking ahead of them with a file in her hand. Gareth won't look at Miranda. He goes across to the window and looks out at the car-park instead.

Dr Jenner pins the X-ray to the screen. He's explaining things, but Fran can't take any of it in. It's a shock to see Jasper's skull on the screen. Somehow you slip into thinking that skulls are figments of the imagination. Long-lost murder victims in crime series on the telly, gruesome toys for Hallowe'en. This isn't happening. There's a dressing over the wound now, and it's stopped bleeding. Fran bends down, puts her mouth against his silky hair, feels the heat of his scalp, smells Johnson's baby shampoo, blood, disinfectant, the suntan oil on her arm.

Dr Jenner's asking why she hadn't taken Jasper to the doctor when he fell over at the Metrocentre. Fran tries to explain he was all right, not sick, not drowsy, not any-thing, running round playing, she hadn't felt justified in bothering the doctor. He didn't lose consciousness then?

'No,' says Fran. And then, 'I wasn't there.'

'You weren't there again today.'

Fran's beginning to feel she's on some kind of short-list for the World's Most Absent Mother prize. It isn't fair. She gave up work to look after Jasper. And Nick can't help because – Fran feels a slow stir of anger – because

Nick bloody well wasn't there either. Nick hasn't been *there* very much at all recently.

'So who was?' Dr Jenner asks.

'Who was what?'

'Who was there when the accidents happened?'

Nick says, 'Gareth.'

'And Gareth is?'

'Fran's son. My stepson.'

'And he was there on both occasions?'

'Yes.'

Fran thinks, No, he doesn't mean that. 'You're saying they weren't accidents?'

'No-o, I'm saying . . . Perhaps it might be a good idea if you didn't leave him alone with his brother.'

'What do we do now?' Nick says.

'Well, he's going to need stitches.'

Fran says, 'Can I stay with him?'

'Of course. I'll just go and find a nurse to help me.'

After he's gone they sit in silence, each finding it hard not to look at the brightly lit skull on the screen. It doesn't seem to connect with the little boy who sits on Fran's knee, cheek pressed into her breasts, sucking his thumb and pulling at his ear. His face is dirty, tear-stained. Fran remembers bending over his bed after that disastrous trip to the Metrocentre. It seems so obvious now she should have called the doctor, got the full story out of Gareth, kicked up a tremendous fuss. They wouldn't be here now if she had. Hindsight's a cruel teacher. She has to remind herself forcefully that, at the time, calling the doctor out to a slight graze would have seemed like the action of a fussy, over-anxious, hysterical mother. But then she was stretched to the limit that day, she'd been only too happy to pretend everything was all right.

Jasper's quiet, too quiet, though at least he hasn't been sick again. Fran clings to the few reassuring things Dr Jenner said. No fracture, that's the main thing. No sign of haemorrhage. They just have to be careful. Watch out for drowsiness and sickness. Jasper looks drowsy at the moment, but then he's had a hard day. This is the time he would normally have a nap. Even the vomiting – he doesn't need a blow on the head to be sick in the car. He does it all the time.

They'll just have to wait.

'I shouldn't've gone to sleep,' Fran says.

'Neither should I.'

'No, well, you were tired. You've had Geordie to look after.' She doesn't bother to disguise the bitterness, though up till now she truthfully hasn't minded. She's always accepted that, however peculiar it might seem to other people, this is something Nick has to do. But now, with Jasper's blood stiffening on her fingers, it looks a bit different. A grown man chasing after his grandad and his auntie, leaving her with a house to run, shopping, cooking, kids to look after, one of them his daughter, for Christ's sake. She's stoking her anger deliberately, because it helps her forget how frightened she is. 'It wasn't an accident,' she says slowly. 'Was it?'

'We don't *know* that.' Nick gropes for the right words. 'Don't think about it. Let's just get this over first.'

It could still be an accident, Fran tells herself. Some bizarre game of Gareth's gone wrong. Twice.

Dr Jenner comes back with a nurse, who's carrying a kidney bowl and scissors. As soon as Jasper feels the scissors in his hair, he screams, and he goes on screaming through all the washing, clipping and stitching that follows.

Outside in the waiting room, Gareth wriggles on his chair, looks up and finds Miranda staring at him again. 'What you looking at, shit-face?'

'You.'

She goes back to her magazine. Ten minutes later Nick comes out, followed by Mum with Jasper in her arms, and says they can all go home.

FIFTEEN

As soon as Nick unlocks the front door, Gareth pushes past him and runs to his room. Fran takes Jasper upstairs, hoping he'll have a nap, while Nick makes sandwiches for the older children. Bag of crisps each, and they can eat it in front of the telly.

Through the open window he hears children's voices. An indistinct murmur and then a girl's voice: 'I wasn't there.'

Upstairs, Miranda lies on her bed, stretched out with her hands on her tummy. She doesn't move even when there's a knock on the door. 'Come in,' she calls, expecting it to be Dad.

Gareth sidles round the door.

'What do you want?'

'You won't tell them, will you?'

'Tell them what?'

'About Jasper.'

She goes still. 'What about him?'

'You know.'

'No, I don't. I wasn't there, remember?'

'Yes, you were.'

'Gareth, I wasn't.'

'You were on the cliffs.'

'Watch my lips. I wasn't there.' She sits up and swings her legs over the edge of the bed. 'Though you do realize, don't you, you've just told me what happened? If I didn't know before, I do now.'

'You'd better not say anything.'

'Oh, go away.'

When he's gone, Miranda lies down again, on her back with her eyes closed, but it's no use. Jasper's face with the eyes full of blood floats on the inside of her lids. I wasn't there.

Lying cunt, cow, sod, bitch, slag. She's saying that now, but when the time comes she'll drop him right in it.

He tips all the old toys out of the carrier bag, and lines them up around his bed, facing the door. Then he realizes some of them should be facing the window, so he has to arrange them all again.

He's only just finished when Mum comes in. She sits on his bean bag and holds her arm out for him to come and sit beside her. There's a deep red crease on her cheek where she's been sleeping in an awkward position. He expects her to be angry, but she's not. Or not on the surface.

Fran knows she should leave it, for tonight anyway,

but she can't go to bed without knowing. 'Do you want to talk about it?' she asks.

'About what?'

'What happened on the beach.'

'Jasper falling over, you mean?'

'Yes.'

'There's nothing to talk about, he just fell over. I told him, Jasper, mind what you're doing, the rocks are slippy, but he wouldn't listen 'cos he wanted to sail his lolly sticks, so he went on to the big slippy rocks and he fell.'

'The trouble is, you see, the cut on his head, it's not in a place where you could knock yourself very easily, just falling down. It's, well, it's right on the top of his head, and if you think of falling down, well, you don't fall on the top of your head, do you? But if somebody was throwing stones —'

'Are you asking Miranda all this? You're not, are you? I get the blame for everything.'

'Miranda wasn't there.'

'Yes she was. She was on the top of the cliffs.'

'When?'

'When it happened.'

'When what happened?'

'When he fell.'

'A lot of people throw stones, Gareth. You and Nick play that game, don't you, when you try to hit a beer can.'

Fran waits, watching the play of expressions on Gareth's face.

'I might have chucked some stones in the stream.'

'Big stones?'

'No.'

'Pebbles?'

'Yeah, pebbles.'

'But one of them hit him.'

No answer.

'Didn't it?'

Gareth starts to cry. 'I wasn't aiming at him.'

'So what happened?'

'I don't know. He just sort of ran . . .'

'You threw the stone and he ran into its path?'

'Yeah.'

'So why didn't you tell us?'

'I thought you wouldn't believe me, I thought you'd think I'd done it on purpose, I always get the blame for everything, I thought you'd think I'd done it deliberately, but I never, honest I never, I was aiming to miss –' He's wailing. Suddenly he jumps up and shouts, 'You're saying I did it on purpose, and I didn't.'

'Gareth –'

Fran tries to get hold of him, but he wrenches himself away, and starts revolving along the wall, clawing pictures and posters off it, till he crashes in the corner and lets himself slide down to the floor, where he lies, kicking his legs and jerking his head from side to side.

Nick appears in the doorway.

'It's all right,' Fran says.

'What's –'

'Please, Nick.'

He goes out again, though not before she's seen how angry he is. All right, I shouldn't be doing this tonight, she thinks. But if they're going to go on living in this house together, they have to try and understand what happened. She still doesn't believe Gareth. Throwing pebbles in the stream is one story; 'I was aiming to miss' is the beginning of another. But she won't get any further tonight.

'Come on, now,' she says, bending over Gareth. 'It's not as bad as that.'

Gareth's whole body is shaking with sobs, though he hasn't shed a single tear.

'Calm down, now. Come on, calm down.'

Gradually, as she continues to murmur reassurance, Gareth stops gasping for breath and lies still.

Fran stays with him till she's sure he's calm, before going down to the living room, where she finds Nick pouring himself a large whisky. He looks up as she comes into the room. 'What did you expect to achieve by that?'

'I wanted to find out what happened.'

'And did you?'

'Halfway, I think. He was throwing pebbles into the stream. Aiming to miss.'

'To miss the stream?'

'I did say halfway.'

'And that might be as far as you ever get.'

Fran shakes her head. 'I've got to know what happened. I'm going into hospital in a few weeks' time. I can't take Jasper with me. I'm bringing a newborn baby back into the house. How do you think it feels to be told I've got to watch Gareth all the time?'

'You don't have to.'

'That's not what the doctor said.'

'He doesn't know Gareth. You plug Gareth into a computer he's no danger to anybody.'

'But he can't live like that.'

'Why not? He has been.'

They stare at each other.

'You think if he tells you everything it'll wipe out the past.' He puts on a schmaltzy soap-opera voice. '"It's good to talk." Not always. It won't help Gareth to say, "I tried to smash the little bugger's head in because I hate his guts." Even if it is true. And it certainly won't help you to hear it.'

Fran shakes her head. 'We have to know.'

'We? I'm part of this, am I?'

'Of course you are.'

'Only just now I got the impression I wasn't.'

'I'm sorry.'

'Can I talk to him?'

She hesitated. 'Well, not tonight.'

'Tomorrow?'

'I just thought it would come better from me.'

'Oh yes.' Nick flicks his eyes at the ceiling. 'You were making a grand job of that.'

Silence. Nick clinks the ice cubes in the glass. 'You know you've always said Gareth used to drive your boyfriends away, wouldn't let them anywhere near him. I don't think that was Gareth. I think it was you. He's your test-tube baby, isn't he, Fran?'

She winces with the brutality of it. 'No, I don't think so. I could do with a bit of support.'

'Well, I'm tired of being the token father. You've got to decide whether you want me in Gareth's life or not.' Seconds later, Nick's horrified at himself. For somebody who's just accused Fran of bad timing he's putting on a pretty lousy performance. After an awkward pause, he says, 'Look, why don't you have a drink?'

'Your solution to everything, isn't it, Nick?'

'No.' They're on the brink of a major row, one of those awful gut-churning affairs that starts over nothing and drags in everything. 'One glass of wine won't hurt. If it was that bad for the baby the entire French nation would be idiots.'

She smiles slightly. 'All right, go on, then.'

'Red or white?'

'Red.'

In the slight stir of fetching a bottle opener and opening the wine, neither of them hears the front door open and close. They raise their glasses, rather wearily, and toast each other. It's only much later, when Fran goes upstairs to check on the children, that she finds Gareth's room empty, and a note taped to the computer screen.

Gareth's on the river path, legs pumping along. He's making for the railway station hoping he's got enough money to get a train to York, where his grandma lives. If he hasn't, it doesn't matter, he doesn't care where he goes, he only knows he has to get away from Mum before she starts asking any more questions. He could see the disbelief in her eyes. She knows Jasper didn't fall.

Gareth's brought hardly anything with him, a fiver and some loose change from Mum's bedside table and the crawling sniper, who's in his jeans pocket. Gareth keeps putting a hand in to touch him, because he's a sort of friend.

Even if he gets to Gran she'll only ring up and tell them where he is. But that doesn't matter. What matters is that he's got to do something to show them what he wants. Telling them's no use, because they never listen.

The wind crawls over the river, making it go goose-pimply. His arms too. It's getting colder, he wishes he'd brought a coat, but it was so hot on the beach, he thought it would go on being hot. To take his mind off shivering and being cold, he looks up the river, counting the bridges. Redheugh, Railway, Metro, High Level, Swing and Tyne, all their lights reflected in the water. It's getting dark. Crossing the road, he cuts through the back streets to the railway station.

Where the first thing he sees is two policemen. He can hardly believe his eyes, but there they are, and not going anywhere either by the looks of them, just standing there with walkie-talkies crackling on their chests. They can't be looking for him, it's too soon.

He strides confidently across to the arrivals and departures board, but the columns of figures baffle him. He thinks there's a train to York in forty-five minutes' time, but he isn't sure and daren't attract attention to himself by asking. There aren't any other kids his age on their own. He'll be all right for a few minutes, but not for forty-five, if he hangs round that long the police'll start asking questions. Can't go for a coke because he daren't spend any money, can't go into the W. H. Smith's because they'll think he's going to pinch something. Probably the safest thing's to go to the gents and just hang about in there.

'Hello, sonny,' says the man at the next stall. 'You on your own?'

Gareth looks down and thinks, *Shit*, because the guy isn't peeing, he's playing with himself.

'No, me dad's in the short-stay car-park.' A glance at his watch. 'Christ, he'll murder me.'

Gareth zips up and gets out of there so fast he practically leaves scorch marks on the tiles. It's like Digger's brother said: 'I'll be buggered if I let a pervert poke my bum.'

Everybody laughed when he said it and so did Gareth, though it took him a week to get the joke.

Ticket office. There's a woman in front of him and she's taking ages. Gareth's jogging up and down as if he wants to go to the toilet, which he certainly doesn't. At last she folds a fiver into her purse, fumbles her tickets off the counter with big clumsy pink fingers and goes. Thank God.

'How much is a single to York?' Definitely a single. No way is he ever coming back.

'Nine pounds, eighty pence,' the woman says.

'Half fare?'

'Yes, half fare.' A shrewd look. 'Does your mum know where you are?'

''Course she does. I'm going to see me grandma next week. Me mum wasn't sure what the fare was.'

Again Gareth gets out as fast as he can. He's running out of the station when he bumps into one of the cops. A solid wall of black chest with crackles and voices coming out of it.

'You all right, son?'

'Yes, I'm just going home.'

They look at each other. 'All right, mind you do.'

Gareth doesn't stop running till he reaches the river and by that time he's so out of breath he feels sick. He bends double like runners do when they've lost a race and waits for it to pass. So far running away's been a total failure. Probably he'll just go home. He's not giving in, though, he's only going back to plan and do it better next time. But he goes slowly, dragging his feet.

The river's on one side of him, the fenced-off works on the other. There are pictures of Alsatians on the tall railings, which are surmounted by coils of barbed wire. The wind whistles between the boarded-up buildings. He finds a stick and drags it along the wire, trying to make the Alsatians bark, but there's no sign of them. The street lamps are on, but there are still patches of intense darkness that Gareth withdraws into whenever he hears somebody coming, but they're on the main road. There aren't many people. Everybody's in their homes or in the town centre. Nobody lives down here. Shot Factory Lane, he reads on a street sign, and turns into it, more to find out where it leads than because he thinks it'll take him nearer home.

When he was running away he felt as if he could walk for ever, but now he's going back his legs ache. He sits down on the kerb, takes the sniper out of his pocket, winds him up, and sets him crawling. He can't crawl very well over the cobbles, he likes the rough ground, but the spaces between the cobbles are too big. Gareth finds a patch of gravel in the entrance of one of the works and lies down to watch. The sniper stops almost immediately. Gareth winds him up again, being extremely careful not to overwind, keeping his ear close to the belly so he can hear the exact moment to stop.

He puts him down, kneels beside him and is just about

to slide down and rest his cheek on the ground when he sees he's not alone. There's a girl, standing with her back to the wire, watching him. A girl with a long skirt and hair down past her shoulder, and as soon as he sees her Gareth knows this is the girl he saw on the cliff. She can't be here, it's not possible.

He feels like a rabbit caught in the headlights of a car. It seems safer to pretend nothing's happening, to stay where he is, and anyway he can't run. Can't run, and there's no point. She wouldn't have to run to catch up with him again. He pretends to be watching the sniper and his tongue feels big and dry inside his mouth, the way it did on the beach, and the moment doesn't pass. Goes on. And on. He waits for the next tick of his watch, and it doesn't come.

No point taking the car. He won't dare park it anywhere, and it's easier to go on foot. Nick cuts through the estate – deserted – then crosses the main road and runs down the slope on to the riverside path. Here the wind howls through gaps in boarded-up factories, and thrums on the barbed-wire fences that surround them. Scraps of polythene, paper, cloth, all kinds of wind-blown debris, caught on the barbs, snap as gusts of wind shake them, go quiet, snap again. Like the irregular thudding of his heart, extra systoles, little peaks and troughs of anxiety traced out on a cardiograph of barbed wire.

He's frightened, and the more he thinks of Gareth

wandering round this area at night the more frightened he gets. Gareth's not a street-wise kid. He thinks he is, because he spends all day playing *Street Fighter* in his bedroom. He wouldn't last five minutes with some of the kids on this estate.

Fanshawe's empire this, shrunk to insignificance. There's his name in blistered paint on a notice-board inside the gate. And more barbed wire. Nick's never seen wire like it, the barbs must be six inches long if they're an inch. Anybody trying to get through that would be ripped to shreds. Still no Gareth. He'll just go to the end of the lane and then turn back. Sooner or later they're going to have to face telling the police.

Nick rounds the corner and sees a child's body lying on the ground at the far end of the lane. He breaks into a run, then slows down, heart bulging in his throat, as Gareth sits up and turns towards him.

'Where on earth have you been?'

Gareth says nothing, just starts to cry.

Behind him the little soldier, face blank and resolute, crawls out of the circle of light into the dark.

SIXTEEN

Miranda lies stiffly under the sheets, as if she needs some-body's permission to move. She hears Dad's heavy steps on the stairs, followed by Gareth's, lighter and quicker. A murmur of voices. She can't hear what they're saying. Something's going on, but she can't be bothered to get up and find out what it is.

The curtains are open, and the speckled glass glows where the moon catches droplets of rain. Miranda gets out of bed and looks out over the garden. It's raining hard now, there's a smell of roses and damp earth. She gulps the cool air down. It's difficult to recapture the heat of the beach that afternoon, the hard brightness, the sharp edges of shadows on the sand.

Toiling across the sand carrying the bag, she'd become aware of a dull ache in her back. Period trying to start. Her whole body felt bloated; if you'd stuck a pin in her, water would have poured out. She was glad to sit down, though when she said she felt tired Fran snorted, 'At your age?'

Fran's ankles were swollen. When she dug her fingers in to show Dad they left pits in the skin that didn't spring back into place like flesh normally does. Fran sat and watched the hollows in her flesh, while Dad fussed about with towels and the sunshade.

Miranda did what she knew she was expected to do and started to amuse Jasper, who was fractious from the heat. The little tendrils of hair on the nape of his neck and round his ears were several shades of gold darker than the rest of his hair. He was supposed to wear a sun hat, but he wouldn't. He kept pulling it off and throwing it away. She showed him how to make a tower and stick a lolly stick in the top as a pretendy flag, but he used the stick to knock the tower down, and then cried because he hadn't got one. Sighing, she shovelled sand into the bucket, and started again.

Dad said he was going to get ice-creams. Did she want one? Yes, she said, though she didn't know if she wanted one or not.

A shower of sand spattered her hands. She looked up through a tangle of hair to see Gareth grinning. Fran told him to go away. He wandered off, straight-backed and mutinous, kicking sand to show he wasn't bothered.

A minute or two later Miranda looked up the beach and saw Dad walking carefully towards them, pausing to lick the backs of his hands where the ice-cream had melted.

Miranda ate hers quickly, stuffing it into her mouth, then said casually that she thought she might go for a walk. She needed to get away from them to think and didn't wait for a reply before setting off. There was no reason, she told herself, for her to spend the entire afternoon playing with Jasper. She was fed up with everybody assuming she liked children just because she was a girl, or that she loved Jasper just because he was her half-brother. Dad would never have left Mum if Fran hadn't got pregnant. That's what Mum says anyway.

The sun was hot on the nape of her neck, her armpits and groin itched, she felt heavy and sullen, as tense as those fat pods of honesty that pop the moment you touch them. She started to climb up the cliff path, hoping for a breeze. The sea was a thin glittering line, far out. No murmur of waves, but there was a constant high-pitched whine, some sort of insect, but to Miranda it seemed that this was the noise heat made.

At the edge of the path there were daisies and poppies. She picked one of the poppy heads and split the rough green outer casing open to reveal tightly furled moist petals, which she tore slowly apart. Red and wrinkled, like a newborn baby's skin. Dad took her in to see Jasper when he was only a few hours old. The petals were sticky. She rubbed her hands and let the shreds drop.

She sat down and looked back at Dad and Fran. How

far away they were and how tiny, as if she were seeing them through the wrong end of a telescope. One day, she thought, she'd remember seeing them like that. When she was old, and it was raining, she'd look back and think how happy she was today, because she was young and the sun was shining and Dad was still alive. And none of it would be true.

She stretched out, wriggling till she found a comfortable spot for her shoulder blades, and let the sun dissolve the pain.

And the next thing she remembered was hearing Jasper scream. Gareth's got it all wrong. She wasn't there.

It's two o'clock before Nick and Fran go to bed, and then there's a last-minute argument over who sleeps where. She wants to sleep in Jasper's room. Nick says, No, she's tired she needs her sleep. *He*'ll sleep in Jasper's room. 'You won't wake up if he cries,' she says. 'Of course I will,' he says. 'I always do.' At last she gives in. He makes up the bed, in darkness in case Jasper wakes, and crawls between the sheets. He's exhausted. How can he not sleep?

He dozes. Once he turns to snuggle into Fran's back, but his groping fingers reach out into emptiness. He feels the edge of the mattress, and wakes more fully. Moonlight streams through the open curtains on to the duvet, which darkens as a cloud passes over, then whitens again. Nick heaves himself on to one elbow, and sees Jasper in that

216

typical baby position, both arms raised above his head, fists curled over on themselves.

He doesn't want to think about yesterday, but the memories come in flashes. Gareth kicking sand into Miranda's face, his stiff-legged defiant walk as he strode away, then slumberous darkness and peace in the patch of shade. Waking up to longer shadows and a cool breeze goose-pimpling his bare chest. No Jasper. Already afraid, staring up and down the beach. The glittering sea and the empty sands seemed to prepare a bowl of silence into which the scream fell. Running along the beach, thigh muscles pulling, feet clogged, like the worst dreams you can remember. Fran, hopelessly far behind, holding her belly in her two hands as she ran. The screams get louder as if Jasper's coming towards him, though he can see him now and he isn't moving, he's lying on the ground. And then, in a rush, blood streaming down Jasper's face into his eyes, into his open mouth. Bare chest registering wet cold and slime, fingers pushing back sticky hair, trying to see the size of the wound through perpetually welling blood. Fran comes up snatching air through a gaping mouth and takes Jasper from him. He sees Gareth climbing down the cliff face, clambering cautiously over the big rocks at its base. How pale and still his face is. The sun flashes on his glasses as he turns.

No Miranda. He can't remember where Miranda was.

The moonlight lies on the floor as white as salt. He turns over, wrestling with the too-tight sheets until he's pulled them loose and wrapped them round his body to form a friendlier nest. That was a good talk they had downstairs. He's amazed at Fran. As soon as Gareth said he'd been running away to York, to his gran's, she seemed to reach a decision. Tomorrow she's going to ring her mother, take all three children for a day out in York, and then, if her mother agrees – and she will, she adores Gareth – he'll stay. Of course it's not as simple as that. There's packing to be done, schools to visit – but in principle Fran's taken the decision. 'You can come home for weekends,' she said. 'Yes,' Gareth replied, with no noticeable enthusiasm. Nick said almost nothing, just let them talk. He's trying very hard not to be pleased. Alternate weekends, he thinks. They'll do a better job with both Gareth and Miranda if they don't have to cope with the two of them together. The reality is, somebody else will be doing the job. But that can't be helped. He and Fran need time together with their shared children.

Sleep. He'll go to see Geordie tomorrow. It's only been two days, but already it feels like a long time. He needs to see him again, not for Geordie's sake, or Frieda's, but for his own.

Jasper snuffles and stretches, settles himself down again. Nick manages to drift off into a sleep that's light at first, translucent, full of flashes of sunlight on water, but then, abruptly shelving, becomes heavy, dark and deep.

★

When he wakes again, he knows he's heard a sound. He strains to listen, but there's only the snuffly sound of Jasper's breathing. He feels the sickness that comes from being abruptly roused from a deep sleep. He gets up and pads across to the door, goes out on to the landing, stands at the head of the stairs, looking down into the hall.

All around him the house is sleeping, muffled in a thick pelt of darkness. Fran's snoring slightly. He hears her turn over, muttering in her sleep. 'Jas −?' but the name disappears into a gobble of smacked lips.

Nothing. He goes into Jasper's room, and climbs back into bed, between the cooling sheets. He's just about to settle down when he hears the sound again. Somewhere in the house a door opened and closed.

Footsteps climb the stairs. He waits, not moving, expecting the steps to go past, but they don't. They stop on the other side of the door. Breathless now, he watches the handle turn.

A girl comes into the room. A girl in a long white nightdress, her hair hanging down around her shoulders. Miranda of course. After the first thud of his heart, he thinks, Who else? She doesn't look at him, but turns and goes towards the cot.

He has to stop whatever's going to happen next. Or rather he has to shield himself from ever knowing what it is. He says, 'Miranda.' She doesn't turn to face him, even then. Moving quietly forward, he sees that her hand's on Jasper's face, covering his nose and mouth, not cutting off the air, more as if she's exploring his face, trying to identify him from touch alone. Nick says again, 'Miranda.'

She turns to face him then, her eyes wide and brilliant in the white light, but though they fasten on his face there's no change of expression, no recognition, and with a chill of fear he realizes she's asleep. He stares at her, tries to swallow. She seems to be aware of his presence, or at least she's aware of somebody's presence. 'I didn't do it,' she says, her voice slurred. 'I wasn't there.'

He has to end this – already the moment seems to have lasted years – but he daren't wake her. He stretches out his hands, and grips her shoulders. Only the thinnest possible layer of skin seems to cover the bone, and she's cold. Colder than the warm September night can possibly account for. He'd have said it was impossible for him ever to feel revulsion from Miranda, but he feels it now. He takes her in his arms and presses her unyielding body against his chest.

He has to say something to close the terrible eyes. Gripping the icy flesh between his hands, he says, 'I know you didn't. Look at me. I know it wasn't you.'

As he continues to hold her, the strained look starts to leave her face. Its lines soften, become more recognizably hers. He's afraid she may wake too quickly and be shocked to find herself here, so he goes on holding her, rocking her, until the greater heaviness of her body in his arms tells him that she's slipped into a natural sleep.

SEVENTEEN

At six-thirty the phone rings. Stumbling downstairs, Nick looks at his watch, can't believe the time. It's got to be Frieda, he braces himself as he snatches up the phone, expecting to hear that Geordie's dead. Frieda shouting into the dreadful phone sounds even more panicky than she probably is. He's not dead, but he's had a terrible night – she's had a terrible night. It can't be long now. Could he possibly come over? 'Soon as I can,' he says. He wonders whether to wake Fran, but she needs her sleep, trailing three children round the Viking centre, then tea with her mother, then leaving Gareth behind, it won't be easy. In the end he writes a note and leaves it propped up against a milk bottle. He'll phone later in the morning before she goes. The streets are deserted. Something about their blankness makes him feel more tired, he's cold, his eyelids prickle, he keeps yawning, leans forward, hugs the wheel.

Frieda's on the doorstep in a pink dressing-gown, looking up and down the street, waiting. Arms tightly folded across her chest, her expression grudging, hyper-respectable, because she's out here, virtually on the pavement, in full view of the neighbours, who for all she knows may be getting glimpses of her nightie.

'He's asleep,' she says. She doesn't know whether to have the doctor back to him or not.

Nick goes upstairs. He is fast asleep, two spots of colour in his cheeks, his nose sharper than before. For his nose was as sharp as a pen and a' babbled o' green fields . . . Well well.

Downstairs, Nick says, 'Why don't we leave it for a bit? See how he goes on.' He makes toast and tea for both of them. When she's finished, he says, 'You go on up, see if you can get a bit more sleep.' 'I can't sleep during the day,' she says. 'Never have been able to.' 'Well, just lie and rest.' Reluctantly, she agrees. Five minutes later, when he goes up to check on Geordie, little whistly snores are coming from the spare room.

Nick lies on the sofa with a coat over him, saying to himself that he won't sleep, he'll just close his eyes. Two hours later, hearing voices, he's struggling to sit up, his brain numbed by sleep.

There's a confusion of stumbling footsteps at the top of the stairs, followed by a sharp cry, a yelp of pain, and Frieda's voice saying, 'Use the bucket, Dad.'

Nick's up and running before he has time to think, taking the stairs three at a time. Geordie's squatting over a yellow plastic bucket which buckles under his weight and Frieda's bending over him, trying to support him with her hands in his armpits.

'Didn't make it,' Geordie said, white-lipped.

Nick takes over, lifting him gently, helping him back on to the bed. Grandad's trying to drag his pyjamas up, more to save the sheet than to hide his genitals.

'Don't worry about that,' Nick says.

The stench from the bucket's terrible. He fetches loo paper, soap and a flannel, and cleans and washes Geordie's bottom, puzzled because the shit on the paper looks like tar. The only thing he's seen remotely like it is meconium. 'All right now?'

It's very obviously not all right. Geordie lies curled up like a foetus, rigid with shame. He'll die now, Nick thinks dispassionately. This is it. He's had his bum wiped like a toddler. He'll die now. And indeed, at that moment, with a gesture Nick can hardly believe he's witnessing, he'd been so certain it was cliché, Geordie turns his face to the wall.

All this time Frieda's been hovering in the doorway, wanting to help, but knowing she's better out of it. That Nick should see Grandad like this is bad enough, but it would be worse for him to be seen by her. Only when it's over, after Nick's drawn back the curtains and picked up the bucket, does he realize it's full of black digested blood.

'Have you seen this?'

Frieda doesn't reply, just whimpers and turns her head away.

'That solves whether we call the doctor or not. I suppose I ought to save some of this for him to look at.'

'Just leave it,' she says.

'No, it'll stink the house out. He only needs to see a bit.'

He carries the bucket to the kitchen, finds a bowl and scoops out a sample. On his fingertips, when he's finished, is a trace of red, mixed in with the black, but only a trace. He covers the bowl and sets it to one side to await the doctor's arrival, then tips the rest down the loo and presses the flush. A swirl of blackness leaves the bowl startlingly clean. He washes and scrubs his hands under the hot tap, dries them on loo paper and throws the paper away. Then he goes downstairs and calls the surgery.

When he goes back, Geordie's propped up against the pillows, their whiteness making his skin look dingy. 'I'm not having any doctor.'

'Too late. I've rung the surgery.'

'Aw hadaway, man, there's nowt he can do. We all know what it is.' He subsides, muttering, 'Complete waste of bloody time.'

He turns away, shoulders hunched, sulky as a parrot. Nick asks about the pain, gets no reply.

Downstairs Frieda's buttering bread. 'I don't want anything,' he says automatically, then thinks she needs it herself and she's more likely to eat if he eats with her.

'No, go on, then. We'll probably feel better if we have something.'

They sit at the kitchen table together. Nick forces himself to take a bite and washes it down with hot sweet tea. They eat in silence. When she's finished she wets her forefinger and reflectively picks up crumbs of bread.

'This is it, isn't it?' she says.

'Yes, he can't survive that.'

By 'that' Nick means not the haemorrhage so much as the humiliating weakness, the exposure. Geordie's a self-contained man in many ways, fastidious, particular about fingernails and underwear. Nick feels he's never known him, not because they've been distant from each other – far from it – but because they've been too close. It's like seeing somebody an inch away, so that if you were asked to describe them you could probably manage to recall nothing more distinctive than the size of the pores in their nose. Only now, when the proximity of death's starting to make him recede a little, can Nick make meaningful statements about him: that he's fanatically clean, that he minds about the state of his fingernails.

After they finish the sandwiches he goes upstairs, but Geordie's asleep or, at any rate, has his eyes closed. Nick bends over him, trying to check from the movement of his chest that he's still breathing. Immediately the blue eyes flicker open and he's subjected to a bright ironical gaze that knows exactly what he's doing and why.

'Not yet.'

The doctor arrives mid-morning, Dr Liddle, a middle-aged man with a vaguely clerical demeanour, Scottish accent, repaired hare lip.

Nick runs upstairs ahead of him and tries to lift Grandad into a better position, but he seems to be hardly conscious, his lips move in protest, his eyes remain closed. Nick doesn't know whether he's getting worse by the minute or whether he's simply decided to close his consciousness against this medical invasion. Not that this is particularly invasive. Liddle raises his eyebrows at the sample, takes Geordie's temperature, his blood pressure, listens to his chest, feels his pulse, looks at the swollen stomach. 'I'm not going to mess him about prodding his tummy, I can see all I need to see.'

Geordie opens his eyes at last, perhaps objecting to being spoken about in the third person. 'It's bleeding again, isn't it?' he says, pressing his hands to the old scar.

'Ye-es, but you've got good healing flesh,' Liddle says comfortably. 'I don't think it'll bleed again.'

No attempt to grapple with the real cause of the haemorrhage. They humour him, all of them, but perhaps that's what he wants. Perhaps in his own way he's humouring them. There's something here Nick can't grasp. Grandad's not a man of much formal education, certainly when forced to refer to bodily functions it's all front passage, back passage stuff, but he's not stupid. His belief that he's dying of this ancient wound may be strange, but it isn't meaningless. The bleeding bayonet wound's the physical equivalent of the eruption of memory that makes his nights dreadful.

'You'll feel a bit weak for a couple of days. Take it easy. We'll soon have you up and about again.'

Geordie seems to find this optimism consoling. He doesn't believe a word of it, but he likes to feel the proper things are being said, a tried and trusted routine adhered to.

'How much pain is he in?' Liddle asks when they're out of the room.

Nick and Frieda look at each other. 'Surprisingly little,' Nick says.

'I'm inclined to leave him at home,' Liddle says. 'As long as you think you can manage.'

Frieda says, 'We can manage.'

'How long do you think he's got?' Nick asks.

'Not long. Days rather than weeks.'

After seeing Liddle out, they go back upstairs and stand at the foot of the bed, looking at Geordie.

'That went off all right,' he says, dismissing Liddle, glad to be alone again.

Frieda tidies round, straightening the sheets. Geordie's tolerant now, letting himself be tidied up, though he rules out shaving, he's too tired at the moment. He'll tackle shaving later. Then he leans back against the pillow, his eyes drooping, but not closed. Nick realizes he's watching shadows dance on the counterpane, leaves with a blue tit pecking about in them, searching for tiny insects. He's lying like a baby will sometimes lie in its cot, entranced by the play of light and shade.

Frieda's searching through Geordie's bureau for his insurance policies.

'Have you found any?' Nick asks.

'Not yet, but they'll be here somewhere. Here, look at this.' She holds up a bundle of receipts. 'He kept everything. Mind you, he was right. They can come back at you.'

'Not after seven years.'

By the time he's washed up and tidied the kitchen she's found the policies, and sits in the armchair, clutching them, looking breathless, excited and slightly guilty. 'I know you might think this is terrible, with the poor old soul still alive, but you've got to be practical,' she says, turning pink.

'I don't think it's terrible at all.'

But she's not comfortable. Every remark about the funeral, who should be told, what Grandad's said he wants done, has to be prefaced by copious disclaimers about not being morbid, grasping, premature, etc. 'He went in for that thing, you know, that scheme where you sort of freeze the cost of the funeral at what it would've been if you'd died at the time you sign on. No matter how long you live it stays the same price.'

'They'll be losing money on him.'

'No, they won't. He's not been in it that long.'

Grandad calls down to them. He's woken up after a long sleep, and Frieda puts the bundle of policies to one side and goes up to attend to him.

While she's gone Nick opens a small drawer in the centre of the bureau, where Grandad keeps family snap-shots, a few letters, his birth and marriage certificates, and his field service postcards. All his letters from France have vanished over the years, but these, for some unaccountable reason, have survived.

NOTHING is to be written on this side except the date and signature of the sender. Sentences not required may be erased. *If anything else is added the postcard will be destroyed.*

After this encouragement to economy of expression, the list of choices.

I am quite well.

I have been admitted to hospital
$\left\{ \begin{array}{l} \text{sick} \\ \text{wounded} \end{array} \right\}$ and am going on well
and hope to be discharged soon

I am being sent down to the base

I have received your
{
letter dated...................
telegram......................
parcel...........................
}

Letter follows at first opportunity

I have received no letter from you
{
Lately
For a long time
}

What fascinates Nick is that word 'quite'. Does it mean 'fairly' or 'absolutely'? In neither sense can it have been an accurate description of the state of the men who, in the immediate aftermath of battle, sat down, stubby pencils in hand, and crossed out the least appropriate choices.

On 2 July, ten days after Harry's death, Geordie was 'quite well'. He was neither sick nor wounded, he had not been admitted to hospital or sent down to base, and he had received a letter from his mother dated the 27th of June.

There are five postcards from then till the end of 1916. In each of them Geordie has crossed out 'Lately' so the final message on each card reads: 'I have received no letter from you for a long time.'

On 14 April 1917, three days after he'd been bayoneted, he's been admitted to hospital (wounded) and 'am going on well' (he nearly died). The address on the other side of the card has been written by somebody else, but the signature, though shaky, is his own. On that occasion too he had not heard from his mother for a long time.

It's almost as if his mother stopped writing to him after Harry's death, or at least wrote very rarely. Perhaps she was so shattered she found it difficult to write to anyone, but a son? And in the front line?

Me mam never got over our Harry . . . Wrong one died, simple as that.

Perhaps it wasn't 'survivor's guilt' that made Geordie imagine his mother had rejected him. Perhaps it was true.

The time wagon travels backwards, pulling them away from the present. On either side figures slip past and vanish: an air-raid warden from the Blitz, an unemployed man in a cloth cap, a First World War officer, his arm raised, cheering, a lady in a crinoline, and so on until the wagon backs into the roar and crackle of flame, shouts, cries, a woman with a wounded baby in her arms, screaming. Leaving her behind, the wagon travels further back, then stops, turns, and moves forward into the light of Viking Jorvik.

Not only into the sights of a fifth-century village, but the sounds and smells as well. A little boy in the wagon behind says, 'Ugh, Mummy, Viking poo,' and everybody laughs.

Mum's fascinated. Miranda's fascinated. Gareth's bored. Jasper's bored too, but since he's on Mum's lap and sucking his thumb he doesn't mind. Looking down, Gareth can see the bald patch where the nurse cut his hair off, and the little barbed-wire ridge of stitches. Everybody says he's getting over the accident really well. And it was an accident. It's fixed in Gareth's mind now, what happened that afternoon, and it won't change. The pebbles he threw will never grow back into stones. None of them will ever connect with Jasper's head.

There comes a time when you're watching somebody die when the sheer tedium of it overcomes you. How much longer, you catch yourself thinking, can this possibly go on? And then you're overwhelmed by guilt because every moment should be treasured.

Sitting on a hard chair in Geordie's room, watching him sleep with open toothless mouth and thin lids stretched across constantly mobile eyes, Nick catches himself thinking, I'll have a bottle of wine this evening. I wonder if there's any cricket on, and then he's ashamed that, even for a second, he could have taken his thoughts away from the dying man. This is one of the last few days, he thinks. The last time we'll ever have together. He tries to whip his tired brain into feeling the seriousness of the events, the preciousness of the last few grains of sand, but his thoughts run into cliché. The fact is that birth and death both go on too long for those who watch beside the bed. The appropriate emotions dry up. You stretch, scratch, ease sticky thighs away from plastic seats, plan forays into the canteen or the kitchen for reviving cups of tea, the chance of a chat. When Frieda comes back with the shopping they giggle in the kitchen like a couple of school kids. Nick's persuaded Frieda to go home for the rest of the day and have a lie down, though she insists on coming back for the night. They each have an unspoken sense that it won't be long. 'I'll just look in on him before I go,' she says. 'I'll not wake him.'

But Geordie feels her presence, the outdoor air on her clothes, and forces his eyes open. 'Hello, Dad,' she says, moving further up the bed. He peers up at her, moistens his dry lips, and says, 'How long does it take for a chap to die?' And immediately Nick's more ashamed than ever, for he sees that Geordie's being spared nothing of all this, not even the tedium. Rather he feels it worse than they do, because for him there's no escape.

After Frieda goes, Nick sits in Geordie's room and tries to make him talk about the past, poking him between the bars of his inertia, as you'd try to rouse a moribund animal. Reminding him of his memories is one way of restoring him, of shoring up the crumbling self. He feeds his own stories back to him. 'Tell us about the time . . . ' 'Do you remember when . . . ?'

There's little response. Either he's given up entirely or all the memories have contracted into a single memory that he's not prepared to speak about. 'Tell me about Harry,' Nick wants to say, but he says nothing. Instead he watches the brown-spotted hand crawl across the counterpane, all that's left of those midnight patrols.

Geordie's too weak now to leave the house. He can't last long, Nick thinks, watching him sink back into sleep.

As you leave the exhibition there's a video screen. Miranda stops in front of it. In the Viking village she'd noticed a man on a barrel gutting fish.

The video tells the story of how they made his face. You uncover a skeleton. From the bones and the teeth you discover the age, the gender and the build of the person it belonged to. Then you detach the skull and put it on a revolving stand, direct a laser beam at it, and feed the exact measurements into a computer, which uses them to produce a three-dimensional model. Select a living person of the same age, gender and build as the skeleton. Dust talcum powder over the face and hair, and then using the same techniques produce a three-dimensional computer model of the head. Then, on the computer, the living person's flesh is wrapped around the bones of the skull. What results is a composite face, but because facial features are determined more by bone structure than by anything else, the resemblance is to the dead person rather than to the living. You are now looking at the face of the past, or as close to it as we can get.

Miranda watches the entire video through twice, then walks, white-faced, through the shop and out of the exhibition into the street, where there are crowds of people laughing, talking, eating, and you need never think about the skull beneath the skin, or the anger that's always on the outside, trying to get in.

EIGHTEEN

'I've been thinking,' Geordie says, sitting up in bed chasing the scrambled eggs he'd requested, with diminishing enthusiasm, around the plate. 'I'd like to see Helen again.'

Nick stares at him blankly. Until this moment he's resolutely refused to see any of his friends, has restricted awareness of the inevitably squalid symptoms of physical decay to his immediate family. Nick's surprised by this sudden desire, distrusts the vivid circles of red on Geordie's hollow cheeks which burn there as distinct and unnatural as a doll's paint. 'All right,' he says cautiously. 'I'll give her a ring.'

Geordie abandons all pretence of eating. Silence. Nick realizes he's expected to get up mid-breakfast and phone Helen now. 'All right.'

Her telephone voice is clear, cool, almost wary, making Nick wonder whom she thought the call might be from, but the tone warms gratifyingly when he says his name, and softens when he mentions Geordie's request. 'On my way,' she says.

'Hey, not yet. Late morning. Eleven-thirty. He needs a couple of hours to pull himself together,' he explains apologetically. 'He's looking a bit rough.'

'All right. Eleven-thirty. See you then.'

As soon as Nick repeats this, Geordie's eyes go to the clock, counting.

'I thought we might change the sheets,' Nick says, not relishing the prospect.

'No, I'll come down.'

'Are you sure?'

''Course I'm sure. And get some fresh air into the place.'

In spite of all Frieda's efforts the house smells of his sickness. Another thing Nick's been hoping he didn't know.

The next two hours are spent on Geordie's *toilette*, getting him dressed, pushing the frail limbs into tubes of cloth which suddenly seem as inflexible as corrugated cardboard. 'You're going to have to rest on your bed after this,' Nick says firmly.

'All right.' But he can hardly keep still, squirming about in the chair, while Nick tries to shave him. Why is it so difficult? He uses a razor himself, has never felt comfortable with a dry shave, a legacy from watching Grandad shave himself: the intent gaze, the careful scraping round the curves of the nostrils, the cleft in the chin, the smears of soap dabbed away with the special pink towel, the rapping of the razor against the edge of the enamel bowl. All watched intently, and then, behind closed doors for fear of being laughed at, practised on childish down and disappointingly sparse adolescent hairs. A lot of shared unspoken history's gone into these scrapings and tappings, though it's bloody difficult to reverse the movements on somebody else's chin. At last in desperation he stands behind Geordie, leaning over him, and gets the bulk of it done that way.

'Sweeney bloody Todd,' says Geordie, not relishing the position, head held back, the razor hovering near his throat. He dries his chin himself. 'There,' he says accusingly, pointing at a tiny red stain on the towel.

'I'll put a plaster on it.'

'You will not. I'll have some o' yon pansy stuff you put on your chin.'

Will you indeed? Nick thinks, going to fetch his carefully hoarded bottle of Antaeus.

'Jesus wept,' Geordie says, sniffing it. 'Smells like a French whore's bedroom.'

He often said that in Nick's teenage years, watching Nick getting ready to go out, desperate to impress some girl.

'Were you ever in a French whore's bedroom?' Nick asks.

'Never you mind.'

The doorbell rings. 'I think that's your date,' Nick says, going to answer it.

Helen's looking away from him down the street when he opens the door, so that for a split second he's able to observe her before she turns to him and smiles. She's wearing, instead of her usual jeans and T-shirt, an ankle-length dress made of some dark blue material, the crinkly stuff that doesn't need ironing. He guesses she's made a special effort for Geordie and likes her even better for it. When she turns to face him, he sees she's carrying a big bunch of roses, not the cruelly wired formal drops of blood you buy in a florist's, but floppy open-hearted blooms from the garden. He kisses her and the stalks wet the front of his shirt. 'Come in.'

Geordie's sitting up, incredibly erect, though a few minutes ago he'd been slumped over his swollen belly. The suspicious areas of brightness in his cheeks are more clearly marked than ever.

'Hello, Geordie,' she says, bending over Grandad and kissing him. 'I've brought you these. I didn't know whether to bring you beer instead.'

'No, I don't think I could face beer.'

They sit and chat. Unselfconsciously, Helen holds Geordie's hand, his skin against hers speckled with the fall-out of old age, moles, brown spots, tags of flesh, a raised rough patch of something he needn't worry about now. Her skin's lighter, smoother, though even her hand,

Nick notices, no longer has the unmarked firmness of youth. She must be nearer forty than thirty, and a woman's hands age faster than the rest of her body. Around her wrists are lines where even a few years ago no lines would have been. 'The bracelets of Venus.' Nick dredges the phrase up rather proudly. Since he apparently goes round smelling like a French whore he may as well think like one as well. 'Would you like a drink?' he asks. 'Wine? Or is it too early?'

'Wine would be lovely,' Helen says.

They're chatting together easily and yet intently, still holding hands, and suddenly Nick realizes something that's probably been staring him in the face for years. Geordie's in love with Helen, in love with a woman sixty years younger than himself, hopelessly, helplessly and no doubt at times humiliatingly in love, and has been ever since he met her. This is why he's achieved this minor resurrection from the dead. This is why it matters so much that he should be shaved and dressed, and that the house should not smell of his decaying body.

It seems only right, having had this perception, to leave them alone as long as possible. Nick opens and pours the wine, then withdraws to the kitchen and busies himself tidying up. He doesn't want to think about what he's discovered, doesn't want to drag it through the rag and bone mill of his mind, he's humbled by it and he knows that this is the right feeling.

Meanwhile the flow of conversation from the next

room goes on, too low for him to distinguish individual words. When he finally rejoins them Helen's leaning over Geordie giving him a kiss.

Hours, they'd spent together, taping his recollections of the war and the years that followed. Geordie was puzzled at first by the direction of her questions. He was so used to telling people about the trenches – that's what they always wanted to hear – that it took him a while to understand that Helen was interested in the ways in which, over the years, he's learned to manage his memories. Once he understood, he was interested in her theories, though he always denied that his memories had changed to accommodate changes in public attitudes to the war. 'I wish they did change,' he said, trying to get her to see the perpetual present in which his worst memories existed. Reading the transcripts, Nick had seen it clearly. The wordless, hallucinatory filmic quality of his memories. A flare goes up, illuminating bleached sandbags and tangled wire, but the trembling light never falls. A scream begins and never ends. For Helen, memories are infinitely malleable, but not for Geordie. Geordie's past isn't over. It isn't even the past.

Grandad sips his tea. 'Tastes of iron,' he says to Helen, not complaining, merely making an observation. 'It's the pills.' Then to Nick: 'Can't I have a drop of something stronger?'

Nick gives him a glass of brandy, pours more wine for himself and Helen. Geordie never could get a taste for white wine even at the best of times. 'Virgin's piss,' he called it.

The wind blows rain against the window pane, a spattering of drops that makes Geordie jump. It grows rapidly dark, a storm closing in, the first signs of autumn. A leaf whirls down, and clings for a moment to the glass. Geordie grows more exhausted by the minute, though he's reluctant to give in and let Helen go for what he must know will be the last time. Nick, seeing her now through Geordie's eyes, thinks she would be easy to love.

At last Grandad's had enough. Immediately Helen drains her glass. Nick realizes she doesn't want Geordie to have to reveal his weakness by getting up while she's still there and hobbling towards the stairs. Another kiss, this time on the mouth, and then she's ready to go.

Outside, blinking in the rain, flushed from the wine though she's only had two glasses, she says, 'How long do you think he's got?'

'Not long.'

'He doesn't seem too bad. He's better than I thought he would be.'

'He was holding himself together for you.'

She kisses him and gets into her car. 'Ring me.'

Going back inside, Nick finds, as he'd expected, that Geordie suddenly looks dreadful. The change from a few moments ago with Helen in the room is almost unbelievable. His cheeks are sunken, he won't see Helen again, ever, and the knowledge is written all over him, in the defeated sag of his shoulders, in the way he allows himself to be half supported, half carried to the sofa, where he sinks back against the cushions, refusing even to think about the trek up the stairs. Bereavement's nothing, Nick thinks suddenly, in comparison with the total loss, the absolute bereavement, experienced by the dying. He'll go tonight, he thinks, then immediately disowns the thought. He's said that the last three nights and Geordie's still here.

After a while Geordie drifts off to sleep. Nick finishes the rest of the bottle and then, for good measure, has a brandy. He feels desperate, restless, phones Fran, has a word with Miranda, hears Jasper gurgling away in the background, feels they're a million miles away. A good day in York, and Gareth didn't cry when Fran left. 'Did you?' he asks. Long pause. 'A bit.'

Geordie's stretched out, looking more ill than ever, his mouth slightly open. Nick watches for the rise and fall of the thin chest beneath the shirt, and it's a long time coming. He realizes he's been holding his own breath and forces himself to breathe normally.

The wind howls down the chimney, hurls rain against the window, chases drops diagonally across the pane. He remembers some childhood illness, fever, a sore throat, pain, and Grandad sitting on the bed beside him, watching individual trickles of rain race each other down the glass.

Another childhood memory of bad weather. Grandad saying, 'Pity poor Mary on the wild moor on a night like this.' The words are as evocative as those lakes of orange tea ruffled by his breath.

'Do you want to go upstairs now?'

'Not yet. Why don't we have a proper fire?'

Because, Nick thinks, the rooks probably nested in the chimney last spring and we'll set the whole bloody row on fire. He brings in newspapers, coal and sticks, rakes out a whole summer's worth of fag ends, ash and bits of paper, then, criss-crossing sticks with nuggets of coal on a bed of scrunched-up paper, begins to build the fire. Geordie watches, taking pleasure in the exercise of a simple skill. Nick applies a match to the fans of paper, but the coal's wet, the fire spits sullenly and burns dead. He holds a sheet of newspaper across the fireplace, feeling it sucked in at once by the fierce draught. Rapidly the paper grows yellow, hot and thin. A picture of ruined Sarajevo blackens and begins to burn. Only just in time Nick whips away the page in a gust of sparks and acrid smoke.

When he looks back into the room, Grandad's awake. The firelight, seeking out the hollows of the eye sockets, seems to strip flesh from bone. He's looking at a skull.

'Do you want a pain-killer?'

'Aye, go on, I think I'd better.'

Nick watches the swallowing of water, the cautious placing of the pills on the back of the tongue. It takes three swallows each to get them down, the back of his throat's so dry. 'Do you want some artificial spit?' He sprays artificial spit, as they both call it, round Grandad's mouth. The stuff smells awful and tastes worse, but there's no doubt it adds to Grandad's comfort. He settles back against the sofa cushions and stares into the fire. Nick thinks he might read for a while, though in fact he stares at the newspaper without even trying to read it, since he knows from experience he'll retain nothing. Extreme tiredness seems to demolish concentration, almost like shock or grief or the after-effects of anaesthesia. He can't even locate himself in the week, has to look at the top of the paper to find out what day it is. At last he lets it slip, sighing, to the floor.

Geordie's eyelids are drooping, the pain-killers beginning to work. 'Come on,' Nick says, tossing his cigarette on to the fire. 'Let's get you up to bed.'

He carries Geordie upstairs, and undresses him. Stone cold, Nick thinks, feeling his legs, though the fire downstairs was blazing hot. 'Do you want a bottle?'

No answer. His eyes are closed. Nick fetches his pyjamas, puts them on and slides in beside Geordie. If he can offer nothing else he can offer the warmth of his body. He lies tensely aware of Geordie beside him, reluctant to turn and look at him, willing him to go to sleep. After a few minutes Geordie's breathing becomes deeper, and Nick risks a sideways glance.

At first sight he seems to be asleep; his eyes are slivers of white and his mouth's open, but then, as Nick watches, the tip of the tongue comes out and works its way round his lips to moisten them, and the eyes flicker. He says, and the words cling to his dry mouth, 'I am in hell.'

Nick turns on to his back, and stares into the darkness for what seems to him a long time, until sheer exhaustion presses his face down into smothering folds of sleep.

Waking early the following morning, stiff and cramped, Nick finds Geordie not merely asleep, but probably, he thinks, unconscious. His breathing's laboured, his skin looks flushed, but feels clammy, and even a shake of the arm fails to rouse him.

Nick runs downstairs, phones Frieda and Fran, tries again and again to reach the doctor. When he finally gets through and books a visit he wonders why he's bothering, what he expects the doctor to do that hasn't already been done. Frieda arrives, panting for breath, goes upstairs by herself and comes down again, red-eyed. They stand in the kitchen together, drinking tea, talking about funeral arrangements, half ashamed, wondering whether there isn't something indecent about doing this while Geordie's still alive. St John's, they decide on. Frieda's mother's buried there, and there's room in the grave, though Frieda can't for the life of her remember where she's put the deeds.

The day drags past from breath to breath, each seeming for one shuddering moment to be the last. When Nick takes Geordie's hand there's an unexpectedly strong answering grip. Geordie seems to be trying to pull himself into an upright position. He says, Pull, pull, but it hardly seems fair hauling him into an upright position, when there's nothing to be gained. But ignoring the plea's horrible. Geordie's totally helpless now and yet Nick's not doing the one thing he's asked to do.

From time to time Frieda puts a feeding beaker to his lips, and he drinks eagerly, his mouth puckering round the spout like a baby's on the nipple. When he's finished there's a smear of milk on his chin that Nick wipes away. Then for hours – nothing. Asleep, drugged, unconscious, it's hard to tell – his breath hardly raises the counterpane, and his eyes are closed.

The doctor comes, hooks up the eyelids between thumb and forefinger, shines a torch. A stroke, he says, and for one insane – no, not insane, entirely sane – moment Nick wants to laugh. Bayonet wound, cancer, doesn't matter now. Geordie's sidestepped them both. After the doctor's gone, Nick, remembering something he's heard or read, puts his fingers to Geordie's pulse, and there it is: beat, echo, beat, echo. His breathing's changed too, though Nick would find it difficult to describe the change.

They sit with him, one on either side of the bed, not saying much. At last, just after ten o'clock, Geordie draws a particularly raucous breath, holds it, lets it out slowly. Nick and Frieda look at each other, she leans forward, half in the expectation of relief. Then another breath, and she sits back. They glance at each other and then quickly away, each dreading to see the other's disappointment. Another breath, another pause. They wait. A shudder passes through Geordie's thin chest, a lifting of the ribs. A clock ticks in the silence. No breath and still no breath. Tick. Tick. No breath. 'He's gone,' Frieda says, and, though they've expected this moment for weeks, the words are amazing.

NINETEEN

Downstairs, Nick makes a cup of tea, pours a slug of brandy into Frieda's, and persuades her to drink it.

'I can't believe he's gone,' she says, cradling the cup in her hands. 'It's like the side of the house going.'

'What do we have to do?' Nick asks.

'Nothing, I don't think. Nothing we can do now till morning.'

'I'd like to tidy him up a bit.'

'I can do that.'

'No, let's do it together.'

They get a bowl of water, towels and soap, and go upstairs.

'He was shaved yesterday. I don't think we need to do that,' Nick says.

'No, the undertaker'll do that. Just straighten him out.'

Nick pulls the sheets down, and Frieda looks away while he does what has to be done.

'You'd better put a towel,' she says. 'Sometimes, they . . . You know.'

Nick pushes a clean white towel between Geordie's legs. He feels self-conscious, handling the penis and scrotum as he cleans him up, wondering why he's bothering since Geordie can't be aware of, or care, who does these essential last jobs. But it's right they should be done by somebody who knew and loved him. Right too that they should be difficult to do. Even in death the genitals are a source of power. Frieda's averted face and his own shyness have a truth to them that trivialized the easy acceptance of nudity. He dries the still warm skin, fastens the pyjama jacket, and draws the sheet up to his chin. The eyes have opened slightly, and he presses them closed.

'Do we put his teeth in, do you think?'

'We'd better,' Frieda says. 'He'll have stiffened by morning.'

They force the teeth into his mouth and then Frieda works on it, producing a more natural expression than the faintly sardonic sneer left by the stroke.

'Doesn't he look peaceful?' Frieda says, standing back to inspect her handiwork.

Nick opens his mouth to agree, but at that moment Geordie's voice says in his ear, so loud it's like taking a punch: 'I am in hell.'

His last words, Nick thinks, hoping it's not true, straining to remember something else he'd said afterwards, but he said nothing else, except 'Pull, pull', which hardly seems to count.

'Should we sit up with him?' He's treating her as the

expert in death, though her experience, like his, is limited. The expert's lying in the bed between them.

'No,' Frieda says. 'I think you should try to get a good night's sleep. There'll be a lot to do in the morning. I'll stop here.'

It's now nearly midnight. He's been dead two hours. His forehead's cold and damp, the clammy feel of mushrooms before they're washed.

'Will you be all right?'

''Course I'll be all right,' she says.

'You won't be frightened?'

'What of?' A scornful sniff. 'The dead can't hurt you.'

Fran's asleep. On a sudden impulse Nick walks along the corridor to Miranda's room. She's reading. 'Miranda,' he says.

She looks relieved to see him. 'Dad. I'm sorry about Gramps.'

'Yes, I'm sorry too. Shouldn't you be asleep?'

'I was just going to put the light out.'

'It's late, you know.'

'All right, I'll stop now.'

He leaves her reaching out a hand to the switch.

Gareth next. Only the bed's empty, and for a moment he's surprised, then he remembers that Gareth's staying with Fran's mother.

Jasper. Breathing snuffily, smelling of pee and milk, a warm, animal smell that makes Nick want to rest his face against the tiny chest. Instead he tucks the sheet more snugly round him.

Fran's deeply asleep, but stirs, moving slightly to accommodate him as he slides in beside her.

Nick wakes to find her side of the bed empty, goes downstairs and finds her in the kitchen feeding Jasper soft-boiled egg. They embrace over his noisy gesticulating form. 'I thought I'd leave you to sleep,' she says, a little shy with him, not knowing quite how she's supposed to react. 'Yeah, thanks,' he says, and bends down to Jasper, who knows nothing and is therefore easier. Jasper's holding a soldier dipped in yolk up to him. 'Is that for me?' Nick says, pretending to eat. 'Yum yum yum.'

'Did Frieda stay there?'

'Yes.'

'You should have brought her back here.'

'No, she wanted to stay. I'd better get back there,' he says, looking at his watch. 'We'll need the doctor out, I suppose, and the undertaker.'

'He's going into the chapel of rest?'

'I should think so, but she'll want him home before the funeral. Apparently he wants – wanted – to be buried in St John's. My grandmother's buried there. So I thought we might have the tea here, but you know we –'

'Of course we'll have it here.'

'I mean she'll want him back home before the funeral, but she'll sleep there, I expect. I don't suppose he can be left in the house on his own. Though I don't know why not, give the burglars a shock.'

'Nick.'

'No, he'd like that.'

Nick nibbles two slices of toast, standing with his back to the sink, wanting to be gone. At the back of his mind there's some absurd idea that Grandad's expecting him to walk through the door.

Instead, when at last he opens the front door, a breath of cold air greets him. Of course the windows will have had to be kept open all night. The house sounds emptier and smells different. Frieda's winding up the cord on the vacuum cleaner, having cleaned the living room. She doesn't look as if she's slept much, he thinks, with a stab of compunction, as he bends to kiss her. 'How was it?'

'Quiet,' she says with a roguish twinkle, and they giggle together like a couple of naughty children. 'Will you go up and see him?' she says.

'Yes, all right.' Straightening his face, he goes up, feeling the cold of Geordie's bedroom meet him halfway up the stairs. Geordie's still lying with the sheet pulled up to his chin. Well, of course he is, Nick tells himself impatiently; it'd be a remarkable state of affairs if he'd moved. But then he *has* moved, infinitesimally. The muscles of his face, stiffening, have changed his expression from stern to quizzical, and the eyes have opened slightly so that a line of white's just visible. Nick reaches out to close them again, and the skin feels icy cold, and somehow thicker, which must be a sign of rigor mortis.

It has the curious effect of making Geordie untouchable, as he had not been the previous night, when his body, though cooling fast, had felt little different from his living body. 'Oh, Grandad,' Nick whispers aloud.

The movement of exhaled breath disturbs the dust motes that are sifting about in the shaft of sunlight that comes through the crack in the skimped curtains. The silence receives the whisper and deepens around it. Nobody here, Nick thinks, though he sits for a while longer, taking in the smells, all clean and cold, white sheets, soap, the musty smells of sickness banished, the smell of death mercifully not detectable yet. And then, as he stands up to go, there's another smell: Antaeus. 'Yon pansy stuff you put on your chin.' But Nick's not wearing any, and when he leans forward, putting his face close to his grandfather's, he can detect no trace of aftershave lingering on the skin. There shouldn't be – they washed his face last night. Yet the smell's powerful – nothing vague or tentative about it. You'd think a whole bottle of the stuff had been spilled.

Nick remembers that he's not yet told Helen about Geordie's death and goes downstairs, intending to get it over with as fast as possible. She's on her answering machine. ' . . . and I'll get back to you as soon as I can.' Nick waits for the beep, knowing he won't be able to leave this message on the machine. 'Hello, Helen, this is

Nick,' he says, sounding self-conscious. 'Could you give me a ring?'

The phone's picked up before he's finished. 'Nick.' Her voice sounds incredibly close and breathless.

'Helen.' Faced with her unexpected presence, he's lost for words. 'I'm afraid it's over. Well, pleased it's over, I suppose.'

He hears his voice objectively, as if this is a recorded message and he's playing it back. He finds himself thinking, That man sounds desperate.

'Peaceful?' she asks, obviously detecting his uneasiness.

Nick hesitates. 'Not exactly.'

'I'll be here all day.'

He was wanting her to say that. 'Later this morning? About twelve?'

'I'll see you then.'

The doctor comes at half past nine. He stands by the bed looking down, a younger man than Nick, but used to death as Nick is not. Faced often enough with far worse deaths than this. 'Well, he had a good innings,' he says. Nick agrees. He goes on agreeing, because the neighbour says it too, and then the Vicar. A few old friends come in to see the body, and that's good, because it's the old way, and Frieda thinks Geordie would have liked it. But, at intervals, throughout the day, as startling as gas bubbles bursting on the surface of a pond, he hears Grandad's voice: 'I am in hell.' *Am*. It's the present tense that ambushes Nick now.

They're going in later to choose the coffin. For now, the undertakers arrive with a body bag, and when he looks at this thing, this gleaming black plastic dustbin liner, Nick feels overwhelming anger. He'd imagined a coffin, labouring shoulders, jostling on the narrow stairs, that impressive mixture of extreme physical effort and silent respect, familiar from royal funerals. Instead there's this zipper bag, drawn up across the face. Mind his nose, he wants to say as the zip closes. Stupid – even if they did catch the skin, he wouldn't feel anything.

The body sags, between the men carrying it, into a shallow U. Even a deeply unconscious man would respond to being moved in a slightly different way. There'd be some residual muscle tone to differentiate him from this limp parcel of dead meat which can do nothing to help itself or its bearers. Nick doesn't want to see them carry it downstairs. Instead, he stays in the room, staring at the creased and rumpled sheets which, despite all his precautions with the towel, are slightly stained. He listens to the rustle of plastic, as the shuffling steps recede, thinking that the rumpled bed looks more like the scene of recent love-making, than a place where somebody had died. Again, on the cool air, the scent of Antaeus. Once more, Nick smells the pillows, the counterpane, his own fingertips, but there's nothing there.

After the undertakers have driven away, Nick walks slowly along to the bathroom, where he looks into Grandad's steel shaving mirror. There's a syndrome that consists of an inability to recognize one's own face. Perhaps he's just succumbed to it, for the face that stares back at him is nothing like his own.

It's late afternoon when he stops the car outside Helen's flat and looks up at her window above the trees. There's nobody else he wants to talk to now, nobody else who knows Geordie as intimately as he does. He presses the intercom and announces his name.

A crackle of sound that he hardly manages to identify as her voice tells him to come in. On his way up the four flights of stairs he pauses, not wanting to arrive gasping for breath, and from then on is puzzled by the sound of talking. She has the radio on perhaps, but then one of the voices – a man's voice – starts to sound familiar. It's somebody he knows. He hopes she hasn't got one of their mutual colleagues with her. If she has, he decides, he'll stay the minimum length of time, then make some excuse and leave.

Standing outside the door, hand raised to knock, he recognizes the voice as Geordie's, and feels his skin roughening like the sea when the wind blows over it. Geordie, not dead, not silenced. Geordie, preserved on Helen's tapes for ever. He's singing the song his wife used to sing, to calm him, in the early days of their marriage, when his nightmares soaked her in sweat and she'd wake to find the sheets drenched with his piss.

> Keep yor feet still, Geordie hinny,
> Let's be happy for the neet,
> For we may not be sae happy thro' the day,
> So give us that bit comfort,

Helen's voice joins in.

> Keep yor feet still, Geordie lad!
> And dinnet drive me bonny dreams away.

It's a good moment, and he wonders whether she intended it for him, this reminder that the truth of Geordie's life did not consist of those traumatic memories that erupted to plague his final months, but in the continuity of loving that had filled all the years between.

He needs to know. He knocks, and the door swings open. It's been open all the time.

They're in the room together now, not speaking because the tape's still playing. The song ends in a burst of shared laughter. Helen clicks stop. She's holding herself, as she looks down at the recorder, her face slightly averted from Nick. When she finally turns and raises her face to his, he sees her eyes are full of tears, and, without thinking, opens his arms to her.

They cling together, Helen choking back tears. After a while she pushes herself off his chest and says, unsteadily, 'Drink.'

'I'm driving.'

'You can walk from here. Anyway, one won't hurt.'

Yes, that's true, he thinks, I can walk from here. 'All right.'

The chink of ice in the glass, she knows exactly how he likes it, they've been friends for so many years. Miranda was a baby when they first met. She comes back into the room and hands him the glass. He moves further along the sofa to make room, but, struggling with tears, she shakes her head and goes to stand near the window, a spare dark shape silhouetted against an intricate network of branches. She raises her glass and drinks. The sunlight, catching the cut-glass, dazzles him.

He says, 'He was in love with you.'

A turn of the head. 'Yes, I know.' A moment's silence. Then: 'How was it?'

'His last words were, "I am in hell."'

She waits. Nick realizes he can't – daren't – go on. After a while, he manages to say, 'I want you to tell me about Harry.'

'Yes.' A faint smile. 'I thought you might.'

'You didn't destroy the tape, did you?'

'No, but it wasn't because I was hanging on to it as raw material or anything like that. I couldn't destroy it because it had his voice on it. It's just something you can't do – like tearing up a photograph. It's – you don't do it if you love the person. And I'm sorry I didn't tell you, but he specifically asked me not to tell any of the family. I felt I had to respect that.'

'Do you think you can tell me now?'

'I think *he* can tell you now.'

One tape removed, another inserted. A squeak and gibber of distorted voices, and then Geordie's in the room, as strong and vigorous as he'd always been, until a few short months ago.

> GEORDIE: No, well, you see the idea was you all joined up together – a big crowd of us lads from the factory all went along together, and yeah, I think the idea was it was a big adventure. Not even that really, bit of a laugh. Better than the factory.

A long silence filled with the tape's asthmatic breath. He's in no hurry to talk about this.

> HELEN: So you and Harry were together from the start?
>
> GEORDIE: We were in the same company. They didn't do that so much, after the Somme, they learned the hard way. There were families, whole streets, where the lads were wiped out. After that they split brothers up.
>
> HELEN: Too late for you and Harry.
>
> GEORDIE: Yes.
>
> HELEN: What was it like being together?
>
> GEORDIE: Ah, well, now, what was it like? Well,

you know, Helen, in my young days, men weren't supposed to be frightened. If you were, you didn't own up to it, it was something you were ashamed of. Now it's all gone the other way. The idea now is: everybody's frightened all the time. War, I'm talking about. Trouble is, that isn't true either. Not everybody's equally frightened all the time. There are some men who're – I won't say fearless. But as good as. Because fear to them's like putting petrol in the engine. Harry was like that.

HELEN: Did you mind that?

GEORDIE: No, I was proud of him. In the run-up to the Somme there were these tremendous bombardments, they were supposed to be cutting the German wire to ribbons. And there was this officer in our company, he just didn't believe it. He used to take parties out cutting the wire, he used to say, if I cut the bugger meself I know it's been cut. This night – it was more like a raid than a patrol, they were waiting, their faces blacked up, helmets on, all you could see was the whites of their eyes and their teeth. I patted Harry on the back, and I says, Good luck, Harry. And they all bust out laughing, it was the wrong man. Well, no harm done, give 'em a laugh, but you know ever since – and I can't get this out of me head –

ever since there's a part of me mind that thinks,
If only I'd recognized him, if only I'd said,
Good Luck to the right man, he wouldn't have
died.

Is that all? Nick thinks. One tiny incident magnified by
a lifetime's guilt at having survived. He opens his mouth
to speak, but Helen raises her hand.

> GEORDIE: Jerry twigged it. A flare goes up, all
> hell's let loose. They all come crashing back
> into the trench, and I'm looking from one
> blacked-out face to another, trying to find
> Harry, and they're worse now than they were
> when they set out. It's just lumps of mud,
> walking. One of them's bleeding. 'Where's
> Harry?' And the officer counted them, one
> missing. And after the shells coming over died
> down a bit you can hear this scream, and it
> goes on and on and on. I know I've got to go
> out.

A long silence. When he starts to speak again it's in a
more reflective tone.

> GEORDIE: One thing they drilled into you: you
> don't stop for the wounded, never stop for
> them, doesn't matter who it is, you don't stop.

You don't go back for them, you don't risk your life for them, you don't risk anybody else's life. And of course they'd got to drill it in, because the natural thing is to look after them. You've been living together, training together. But at this stage, you know, we were still innocent. In lots of ways, I think we were. And there was a feeling that with brothers, it was different. You were almost expected to do it. And so when I said I wanted to go out, nobody stopped me. I'm scooping up mud, it's cold, I'm rubbing it on me face and the backs of me hands, and then I'm off. It's like being naked. Out there, I mean. It's like the trench walls are part of your body and when they're not there any more you feel . . . skinned. Harry shouts – I'm virtually sure this is true – 'Don't come out.' But of course I keep going. Just as I'm crawling the last few feet a flare goes up, he's screaming, all I can see is the mouth, little blue slitty eyes, and his guts are hanging out. I touch his leg. He knows I'm there because he goes still. I suppose he might have thought I'd come to take him back. And then he starts screaming again and that's easier because I know I've got to stop him making that noise. I'm crawling up his side, all I can see is the open mouth, and my fingers are digging into his chest, finding the right place and then I ram the knife in and the screaming stops.

Silence. Nick looks at Helen, and sees from her face now how she floundered and groped for words then.

HELEN: It must be terrible to kill somebody you love.
GEORDIE: Yes, it must be.

Helen was closer to the microphone than Geordie. Nick hears the intake of breath.

HELEN: You didn't hate him.
GEORDIE: Didn't I?
HELEN: You said yourself you were proud of him.
GEORDIE: I was proud of him when I was a kid, some of the time. The rest of the time I hated him.
HELEN: But that's a child's hatred, Geordie. Kids are always saying they hate people, they wish they were dead, but they don't mean it. They don't act on it.
GEORDIE: They don't get the chance, do they, most of the time? But —
HELEN: Yes?
GEORDIE: It's not that. You see, when I'm remembering all this, it's like falling through a

trapdoor into another room, and it's still going on. I don't remember the mud on my face, I feel it, it's cold, gritty. And I see everything like that, until I get to Harry's wounds. And then what I see in my mind's eye is something like fatty meat coming out of a mincing machine. And you know I've seen lots of men disembowelled, and it's not like that. It's . . . I know that what I remember seeing is false. It can't have been like that, and so the one thing I need to remember clearly, I can't. Nothing vague about it, you understand. It's as clear as this hand . . . only it's wrong. So how do I *know* I couldn't have got him back?

HELEN: How do you know it wasn't murder?

GEORDIE: Yes, that's it. Exactly that.

Helen presses stop and ejects the tape. Nick says, '"I am in hell."'

'Yes.'

'Do you think that's survivor's guilt?'

'No.' She ignores the spurt of aggression. 'I think it's pretty much what happened.'

'And he was alone with that. There was never anybody to say, "You did the right thing."'

'No, all he had to go on was his own memory. And it let him down.'

'You know that bit about the mud, actually still feeling

it? I think I finally understand something, because I don't remember him saying: "I am in hell." I hear him say it. Quite loud, almost shouting. I was pulling out at the top roundabout, and . . . ' He makes as if to hit himself in the eye. It's easy to tell her about the voice. What he can't tell her about is the scent of Antaeus, though it's been in the room since he arrived, and it's growing stronger by the minute.

She comes closer, and stands looking down at him, clinking the ice cubes round her glass, groping for something to say that will carry some comfort. 'You can't sum up a person's life in their last words. I mean, think of all the people who must have said, "I need the bedpan." Think of George V. "Bugger Bognor."'

They manage a laugh. He looks up at her. Slowly, she puts the glass down. Nick feels a moment of self-doubt. He doesn't know whether it's the proximity of death that's caused this overwhelming lust, or if that's just an excuse. The scent's overpowering now. She places her hands gently on either side of his head, muffling all sounds, all voices, even his own, and then, leaning forward, very gently, her legs between his spread thighs, she presses his head to her breasts.

TWENTY

Nick spends the last few hours before Geordie's funeral tackling the house rose, cutting branches and tearing away handfuls of dead twigs and leaves. It's a wonderful, addictive job, like eating peanuts, and it's not possible to think of anything else at all. He's wrestling with a particularly intractable knot when: 'Careful,' Miranda says, steadying the ladder, and her concern brings him back to himself. 'Fran says it's time to get ready.' 'All right, love. Tell her I won't be long.'

He goes upstairs, changes into his funeral suit, and then goes down to greet the relatives who're coming in the cars to church. They'd decided to leave the coffin lid open, and now he's glad of it, for most of the mourners are old enough to want to observe the custom of saying goodbye to the dead face to face. Nick's reluctant to go into the room himself. He's not sure he can bring himself to search for further changes of expression, but in the end he does. Miranda stands by the coffin stoically lifting the face cloth for each one as they come and go. 'Doesn't he look peaceful?' they all say, because it's what you do say, as conventional a response as wishing a bride happiness. Nick looks at Geordie's face and hears his voice again: 'I am in hell.'

It's accompanied him throughout the five days since Geordie's death, like a cerebral parasite. He wakes in the morning knowing he's heard it in his sleep. He stands by the coffin, resting his hand on the polished wood, and prays for silence.

They all retreat into the kitchen while the undertakers' men take the coffin out, then troop down the drive and into the cars. Driving with Frieda in the first car Nick fixes his eyes on the hearse in front with the pale wooden coffin and its white wreaths on top. Barbara's sent flowers, which is good of her, she needn't have bothered, and there are bouquets of spring flowers from the great-grandchildren.

Walking into church behind the coffin, shuffling slowly along, he's aware of faces. No more than three rows full in the front of the church, but then, leaving a respectful gap between themselves and the family, come the packed rows of neighbours, and friends from the British Legion: the seventy- and eighty-year-olds for whom he'd been a kind of mascot, presiding, ramrod straight, over their increasingly stooped and bowed gatherings.

I know that my redeemer liveth and that he shall stand in the last day upon the earth.

Following the coffin down the aisle, Nick wonders

whether Geordie had believed anything so grand. Somehow the subject of religion never came up. He'd not been able to answer any of the Vicar's questions about Geordie's beliefs. They file into the pew. Nick's relieved when the intoning of these certainties is over, and the hymn begins. In the choice of hymns they'd been on firmer ground. Geordie was a great singer of hymns in the bath, and the more sonorous and resounding they were the better.

Oh God, our help in ages past,
Our hope for years to come,
Our shelter from the stormy blast,
And our eternal home.

He'd have approved of that. As does the congregation, whose, for the most part, frail and quavery voices are buoyed up by the familiar tune.

Beneath the shadow of Thy Throne
Thy saints have dwelt secure;
Sufficient is Thine Arm alone,
And our defence is sure.

Among the memorial tablets lining the north wall is one belonging to a man who'd have gone bankrupt if his contemporaries had believed the last verse. Nick's surprised to see the name Fanshawe, until he reflects that

269

while they lived at Lob's Hill this would have been their parish church, just as now it's his.

> Time, like an ever rolling stream,
> Bears all its sons away;
> They fly forgotten, as a dream
> Dies at the opening day.

An odd thought for a funeral, when everybody's promising to remember for ever, but then again he hears Geordie say: 'I am in hell.' Present tense, the tense in which his memories of the war went on happening. A recognized symptom of post-traumatic stress disorder, a term Geordie probably never knew. Though he knew the symptoms well enough, he knew what it did to the perception of time. The present – remote, unreal; the past, in memory, nightmare, hallucination, re-enactment, becoming the present. I *am* in hell.

But suddenly, as the congregation thunders out the final verse, Nick begins to feel angry on Geordie's behalf. It's too easy to dismiss somebody else's lived experience as a symptom of this, that, or the other pathology: to label it, disinfect it, store it away neatly in slim buff files and prevent it making dangerous contact with the experience of normal people. But suppose, Nick wants to shout at rows of faceless white-coats, suppose you're wrong and he was right. Suppose time can slow down. Suppose it's not an ever rolling stream, but something altogether more viscous and unpredictable, like blood. Suppose it coagulates around terrible events, clots over them, stops the flow. Suppose Geordie experienced time differently, because, for him, time was different? It's nonsense, of course. And just as well, because if true, it would be a far more terrible truth than anything the passage of time can deliver. Recovery, rehabilitation, regeneration, redemption, resurrection, remembrance itself, all meaningless, because they all depend on that constantly flowing stream. But then Geordie's truth had been terrible. Ultimately, for him, all those big words had meant nothing. Neither speech nor silence had saved him. *I am in hell.*

. . . *And our eternal home. Amen.* With a rustling of thin paper, an epidemic of emphysemic coughs, the congregation sits down, and listens to the Vicar doing his creditable best to speak poignantly and justly about a man he had never known.

Afterwards Helen reads the beatitudes, and then they follow the coffin out into the churchyard, and stand around the open grave, the hot sun beating down on to the backs of their necks. Nick's funeral suit is made of winter-weight wool. Within a few minutes he's feeling queasy and wishing the Vicar would hurry up. Miranda's wearing a short black dress. Fran's outrageously bright in raspberry pink, but what can she do? She has no black maternity wear, and it's too close to the birth to buy a new dress. Gareth looks bored, though he wanted to come, apparently. Frieda, perfectly turned out, black from head to toe, looks satisfied and anxious, which means it's gone all right so far, but there's still the tea to come.

The grave's lined with plastic grass, and he's sorry for that. When the time comes he picks up a handful of earth and throws it on to the coffin lid. He sees Geordie's face lifted up as the clods of earth land a few inches from his nose. Don't say it, Nick pleads. Silence. Perhaps he's appeased at last, or merely waiting some more opportune time.

Then it's over. They can go home.

Frieda says, 'It's just as well we got that extra joint,' and so it is, for once the first hush and nervousness are over, they're a hungry as well as a noisy crowd. Miranda goes among them with a tray of drinks and soon port-wine complexions are turning an even richer hue, and the papery skins of old ladies are developing a hectic flush on a couple of glasses of sweet sherry.

Nick talks to some cousins he hasn't seen for years and will probably not see again until Auntie Frieda goes, though Geoffrey, by the looks of him, might go before her. Geoffrey is Harry's son, a frail old man, leaning on a stick. Looking at him, Nick sees a small boy emerging from the Scout Hut, his tummy stretched to bursting point with jelly and custard, boasting to his pal about how much he's had to eat. 'I'd rather have me dad.' And little Geoffrey's face falling, as, for the first time, he connected the treats with his missing father. 'Never knew my father,' he says to Nick, accepting a glass of beer instead of the wine that disagrees with his stomach. 'So Uncle Geordie was always a bit of a hero to me.'

In the womb when Harry was killed. There must be hundreds, thousands, probably, like him, Nick thinks, white-haired sons and daughters of murdered children.

He stands and looks around, proud of his family, proud even of Gareth, who's handing round miniature sausage rolls and politely answering questions from people who don't know where he fits in.

But the heat of the room and the thick suit's making Nick feel sick. He doesn't feel he can remove his jacket, but surely now he's entitled to slip out for a quick cigarette. The buzz of voices dies abruptly as he steps out of the french windows. Groping in his pocket for cigarettes and lighter, he goes round the side of the house where he's least likely to be disturbed. Decaying cabbages, with their flabby, mysteriously runed stalks and thick yellow smell, line the path. He hears footsteps coming round the corner of the house, and braces himself for more condolences, but it's only Miranda.

'I've brought you this' – handing him a glass of beer so cold the glass is sweating. 'You looked boiled, Dad.'

'I feel it.' He doesn't know what she looks like. In the past few days the long hair and skirts have gone. Instead, there's a short, rather jagged hairstyle and what used to be called, in his younger days, a pussy pelmet. Eighteen,

273

that's what she looks like. 'I'll be glad when this is over.'

They sit together in silence for a while. Then: 'I'm going home tomorrow,' she says.

Home. It hurts. 'You will ring me and let me know if there's anything I can do?'

She smiles, irony just perceptible in the depths of her eyes, like the glint of a fish turning. He knows, she knows, there's nothing he can do.

Upstairs, Gareth, who's eaten a sausage roll, is flossing his teeth. As his fingers see-saw the thread between the difficult back teeth, he keeps his gaze fixed on his eyes in the glass. Hanging on a nail beside the toothbrushes, there's Nick's grandfather's mirror, the one he used to use for shaving, though it's made of steel, and makes your face look swollen and blurred. Last night, Nick was telling Gran about seeing Geordie's body taken out in a body bag, and how horrible it was. When Gareth's grandad died, he was sent upstairs out of the way, he wasn't supposed to see anything, but he did. He looked out of the spare room window and saw them humping this black plastic sack, and Nick's right, it was horrible. Gareth spits, and swirls away the pinky splat. Then he replaces his toothbrush, and reaches for Nick's, intending to do the usual brisk rub round the lavatory bowl. Only he feels he can't do that now. He looks at the toothbrush in his hand and returns it to the rack.

Downstairs, the chattering rises to a climax before at last the first few people begin to say goodbye. By responding very loudly, Frieda manages to indicate to everybody that it's time they were off.

Nick follows Geoffrey out to his car, then copes with the rush of people who are suddenly leaving, wondering, as he shakes hands and thanks them for coming, whether all the funerals they attend are as cheerful as this. Probably not. Geordie's death has convinced these seventy- and eighty-year-olds that there's life in the old dog yet. He'd been twenty years older than any of them, and so the pretence of grief was rapidly abandoned. This wasn't mourning for somebody who'd died so much as a celebration of somebody who'd gone on cheating death for years. He turns, hand outstretched, and it's Helen. Kissing her, he's aware of the scent of Antaeus, fading. Not on his chin either – somehow he doubts if he'll ever finish the bottle. He watches her walk away, sifts through his mind for a trace of guilt or regret, finds none. At last, his arm around Fran's shoulders, he can stand in the doorway and wave the last of them goodbye.

Frieda's playing with Jasper in the kitchen. They've become good friends in a short time, these two, and it's just as well since she and Fran have arranged for her to move in at the time of the birth. Life's sorting out, settling down, arranging itself into new patterns. Even Gareth seems happier, amazed to find that at his new school in York computers are on the timetable, in every classroom, one for each pupil.

But for Nick, among all the green shoots, there's still

the ache of loss. And so, when the dishwasher's been loaded, the paper plates thrown away, leftovers wrapped in clingfilm and stored in the freezer, he says, if nobody minds, he thinks he'd like to go back to the church. He's afraid Miranda might want to come with him, or Frieda, but Miranda's got packing to do, and Frieda says she's going to put her feet up and thinks Fran should do the same.

It's not dark, or anywhere near dark, when he gets to the churchyard, but the sun's moved round behind the church, and its shadow lies, thick and black, over the graveyard. Going straight to the grave, he's surprised to find it already filled in, and wreaths piled on top to hide the raw earth. Damp moss, wrapped round the stalks of one bouquet, has dribbled wet through the cellophane of the dedication card, blurring the words: 'In loving memory.'

Nick stands and looks down, then moves along to the grave, a few feet further on, where Grandad's parents are buried, deriving some consolation from his family's long attachment to this place. He finds himself looking for Harry's name, and then remembers.

Restless, searching for some discharge of feeling, and not finding it, he goes into the church. He walks up to the altar steps, footsteps echoing across the marble floor, smelling dust, old hassocks, the odour of piety, but unable to feel anything except a kind of nostalgia for the certainties of faith, and even that's false, for he never came any closer to faith than forced attendance at school assemblies, and those marred by an arrogant childish contempt for his father's hypocrisy.

He goes to find the Fanshawe memorial.

In loving memory of Robert Fanshawe
Born October 11th 1896
Killed in action, July 1st 1916

Also of James Fanshawe
Born August 15th 1909
Died November 5th 1911

If any question why we died,
Tell them, because our fathers lied

A bitter epitaph, though there's nothing surprising about that. Fanshawe had lost two sons, why wouldn't he be bitter? What's strange is the determined linking of the two deaths, the conviction of guilt for both. Unless, of course, he's reading too much into it, and Fanshawe merely intended to endorse Rudyard Kipling's call for more and better arms.

Six weeks since they'd uncovered the picture. Six weeks since Miranda stepped back and said, in that soft murmur that had raised the hairs on the nape of his neck, 'It's us.' Not true, he thinks, even as the covered-up figures rise once again to the surface of his mind. He doesn't regret not telling the family about the Fanshawe murder, because even now he doesn't see how the knowledge would have helped them. It's easy to let oneself be dazzled by false analogies – the past never threatens anything as simple, or as avoidable, as repetition.

On his way out, by the west door, he finds the Fanshawe graves, and pauses to decipher the eroded names. William, Isobel, Muriel, James. He finds himself searching for Robert, but then remembers that Robert, like Harry, isn't here.

He wanders off down the path that leads round the outer perimeter of the churchyard, taking the long route back to Geordie. Some of the graves, here under the trees, are so old the names are hidden by moss. They're forgotten, and the people who stood beside their graves and mourned for them are dead and forgotten in their turn. He remembers the trip to France with Geordie, the rows upon rows upon rows of white headstones, ageless graves for those who were never permitted to grow old. He'd walked round them with Geordie, marvelling at the carefully tended grass, the devotion that kept the graves young. But now, looking round this churchyard, at the gently decaying stones that line the path, he sees that there's wisdom too in this: to let the innocent and the guilty, the murderers and the victims, lie together beneath their half-erased names, side by side, under the obliterating grass.